JOIN THE FUN
IN CABIN SIX . . .

KATIE is the perfect team player. She loves competitive games, planned activities, and coming up with her own great ideas.

MEGAN would rather lose herself in fantasyland than get into organized fun.

SARAH would be much happier if she could spend her time reading instead of exerting herself.

ERIN is much more interested in boys, clothes, and makeup than in playing kids' games at camp.

TRINA hates conflicts. She just wants everyone to be happy . . .

AND THEY ARE! Despite all their differences, the Cabin Six bunch are having the time of their lives at CAMP SUNNYSIDE!

Look for More Fun and Games with
CAMP SUNNYSIDE FRIENDS
by Marilyn Kaye
from Avon Books

And Don't Miss
My Camp Memory Book
*the delightful souvenir album for
recording camp memories and planning activities*

Coming Soon

MARILYN KAYE is the author of many popular books for young readers, including the "Out of This World" series and the "Sisters" books. She is an associate professor at St. John's University and lives in Brooklyn, New York.

Camp Sunnyside is the camp Marilyn Kaye wishes that she had gone to every summer when she was a kid.

Avon Books are available at special quantity discounts for bulk purchases for sales promotions, premiums, fund raising or educational use. Special books, or book excerpts, can also be created to fit specific needs.

For details write or telephone the office of the Director of Special Markets, Avon Books, Dept. FP, 105 Madison Avenue, New York, New York 10016, 212-481-5653.

The Tennis Trap

Marilyn Kaye

AN AVON CAMELOT BOOK

CAMP SUNNYSIDE FRIENDS #12: THE TENNIS TRAP is an original publication of Avon Books. This work has never before appeared in book form.

AVON BOOKS
A division of
The Hearst Corporation
105 Madison Avenue
New York, New York 10016

Copyright © 1991 by Marilyn Kaye
Published by arrangement with the author
Library of Congress Catalog Card Number: 90-93624
ISBN: 0-380-76184-X
RL: 5.0

First Avon Camelot Printing: June 1991

CAMELOT TRADEMARK REG. U.S. PAT. OFF. AND IN OTHER COUNTRIES, MARCA REGISTRADA, HECHO EN U.S.A.

Printed in the U.S.A.

OPM 10 9 8 7 6 5 4 3 2 1

For Olivia Lee Van Houten

The Tennis Trap

Chapter 1

In the arts and crafts cabin, Megan peered over Katie's shoulder. "What's *that* supposed to be?"

"What does it look like?" Katie countered.

Megan wasn't sure. Her eyes surveyed the huge mural the girls were working on. It covered three long tables that had been shoved together. The cabin six girls, along with campers from other cabins, had been working on it for weeks. The mural was going to depict all of Camp Sunnyside, and show campers doing typical Sunnyside activities.

Megan scrutinized the small brown figure that Katie had just drawn. She could make out four legs, a tail, two ears . . . "But there aren't any dogs at Sunnyside," she pointed out.

"It's not a dog," Katie said indignantly. "It's a horse!"

"It is?" Megan asked doubtfully.

"Of course it's a horse! What else would I be drawing next to the stables?"

"Oh." Megan wanted to be kind. "Well, maybe it could be a horse."

"Trina!" Katie yelled.

Trina came around the table and joined them. "What's up?"

Katie pointed to the brown figure. "What does that look like to you?"

Trina stared at it. "Um . . . a large cat?"

Katie threw down her brown marking pen in frustration. "Honestly! Can't anyone around here recognize a horse?"

Erin leaned over from the other side of the table and examined Katie's drawing. "Maybe if we saw something that looked like a horse we'd recognize it."

"Very funny," Katie retorted. She turned to the girl on her other side. "Sarah, what do you think this is?"

Sarah glanced at it briefly. "A horse."

"See?" Katie said triumphantly to the others.

"How could you tell it's a horse?" Megan asked Sarah.

Sarah grinned. "Because I heard Katie tell you that's what it is."

2

Katie sighed. "Okay, maybe I'm not the world's greatest artist. Trina, can you help me turn this into something that looks like a horse?"

"Sure," Trina said, retrieving the brown marker.

"I'm going to get started on the tennis courts," Megan announced. That was the part of the mural she'd been most looking forward to working on. Even though she wasn't any more artistic than Katie, she felt pretty sure this would be the one scene she could draw really well. After all, she spent more time on the tennis courts than anyone else, and she knew every inch of the area.

But just as she was picking out her marking pens, Donna, the arts and crafts counselor, blew her whistle. "Time's up, folks," she called. "See you tomorrow."

"Oh, yuck," Katie grumbled as they began picking up their stuff. "Time for archery."

There were similar expressions on the faces of other cabin six girls. Archery was everyone's least favorite camp activity. Only Megan was grinning. And that wasn't because she felt any different from the others about archery.

"No bows and arrows for me," she gloated.

3

"Don't rub it in," Sarah muttered. "I wish *I* could get out of archery."

"Me too," Erin said. "But not if it meant I'd have to teach little kids tennis instead."

"Well, it suits me just fine," Megan said. "And they're not little kids. They're three girls from cabin four."

"Nine year olds," Erin sneered. "Infants."

"Erin, we're only eleven," Trina reminded her.

Erin tossed her head so her blonde curls cascaded on her shoulders. "Almost twelve. Besides, there's a big difference between ten and eleven. We're practically teenagers."

Outside, Megan waved to her cabin mates, who were dragging their feet as they headed toward the archery range. Megan, on the other hand, skipped all the way back to cabin six to pick up her racket and a can of tennis balls. As she walked down the slope toward the tennis courts, she swung her racket at imaginary balls flying through the air.

This had to be one of the most brilliant ideas she'd ever had—and she was amazed she hadn't thought of it earlier in the summer. It hit her just two weeks ago, when she was playing tennis with her friend Stewart, who was visiting

4

from Camp Eagle across the lake. She'd beaten him soundly, and three younger girls who had been watching them applauded. Afterwards, they surrounded Megan, heaping compliments on her. They were all into tennis, they said, and they wanted her to give them some tips on playing better.

So Megan had gone to Ms. Winkle, the camp director, to ask if she could give tennis lessons to interested campers. She was happy when Ms. Winkle gave her permission. And she was thrilled when Ms. Winkle said she could give the lessons during archery period. Not only would Megan get to spend more time on the courts and help younger players, she could get out of her least favorite activity!

Leslie, Polly, and Carla were waiting for her just outside the court. Seeing them, Megan had to admit she agreed with Erin in a way. She felt much older than these kids. "Hi, guys," she greeted them.

Redheaded, freckled Polly leaped up from the bench. Carla, a solemn-looking girl with huge eyes, smiled shyly, while fair-headed Leslie put her hands on her hips and tapped her foot. "We've been waiting for you," Leslie complained.

"Not even a whole minute," Polly assured Megan. "What are we going to work on today?"

"We're going to keep practicing ground strokes," Megan told them.

"But we've been doing that for three days," Leslie whined.

Megan grinned. She'd grown accustomed to Leslie's whining, and it didn't bother her. Well, not too much. "And we'll keep on practicing till everyone's got it right," she said.

Leslie sniffed. "What's so special about ground strokes? That's the most common stroke there is."

"That's why you have to be really good at it," Megan told her. "Since you'll be using that stroke more than any other."

"But I want to work on my serve," Leslie argued.

Megan was beginning to lose patience. "We'll get to serving later."

"I don't mind practicing ground strokes," Carla said softly.

"Then let's get to work," Megan ordered. "We're wasting time talking."

"Sounds good to me," Polly said cheerfully.

Megan beamed at her. She tried not to have favorites among her three students, but it was impossible not to like Polly best. Maybe that was partly because Polly reminded her a little of herself, with her red hair and freckles. Not to mention the fact that she was the most enthusiastic of the three. Carla was sweet and a hard worker, but she didn't have the same kind of spirit. And Leslie could be a real pain.

"Okay," Megan said. "Let me see your grip."

She examined the way each girl was holding her racket. "Carla, that's too tight. Spread your fingers a little. Polly, let your thumb touch your middle finger. That's right. Now, make sure that you start your backswing early enough, the second the ball strikes the ground."

"*I* knew that already," Leslie said.

Megan sighed. "Okay, if you know so much, let's see you hit one." Polly and Carla went off to the side, and left Leslie standing alone. Megan went to the other side of the net, tossed up a ball, and slammed it across the net.

Leslie went into her swing too late. By the time her racket met the ball, there wasn't enough power in her swing to get it across.

Megan ran back around the net. Leslie was biting her lip, and Megan could tell she was embarrassed. She smiled kindly at the younger girl. "What do you think went wrong there?"

Leslie's voice was glum. "I didn't start the backswing early enough. And I wasn't far enough back from where the ball hit the ground."

"Good," Megan said with approval. "Recognizing what you're doing wrong is the first step you can take to learn how to do it right."

Leslie gave her an abashed smile. "Yeah, maybe I do need to work on this a little more."

She wasn't really a bad kid, Megan decided. Just a little obnoxious. She beckoned for the other two to rejoin them. "Okay, everyone. Let me see how you're going to stand." The girls got into position, and Megan looked them over.

"Carla, loosen up. Leslie, bend your knees a little. Now, Polly, you go serve and I'll watch these guys. Then you'll switch places."

As she watched each girl do her ground stroke, Megan thought about how different they were in their playing skills. They all knew the basics of tennis. But Carla was tense and nervous, clutching her racket as if she was afraid someone was about to grab it away from her.

Leslie wore an expression of grim determination. She approached each ball as if it was an annoying fly that she wanted to swat.

But watching Polly was a pleasure. She was

8

a natural, Megan decided. She had good concentration, her strokes were sure, and her movements were graceful. More than anything else, Megan appreciated the expression on her face. She was reminded of a home video her father had made last year of herself playing tennis. Polly's expression was exactly like Megan's had been—exuberant and expectant.

As each girl hit her ball, Megan called out comments. "Good, Polly. Carla, run out and meet the ball. Don't be afraid, it won't bite you. Leslie, keep your wrist firm."

She wasn't really watching their serves very closely, since that wasn't what they were working on. But she couldn't help noticing how weak Carla's were. And when Carla was on the returning end, Megan found herself calling out the same criticisms over and over. Carla's ground strokes weren't showing much improvement. And the poor kid was looking miserable.

After twenty minutes, all three girls were starting to look a little weary. "Time for a break," Megan announced. She gathered with the girls on the bench.

Despite the sweat on her brow, Polly was still bursting with enthusiasm. "This is great! I can actually feel myself getting better and better."

Carla gazed at her in wonderment. "You can? I don't think my stroke's getting any better at all."

"It will," Megan promised her, hoping her tone carried more confidence than she was feeling. She was beginning to wonder if Carla would ever show any improvement.

"I'm as good at this as I'm going to be," Leslie stated with conviction. "So I think we should move on to the backhand."

Polly looked at her reprovingly. "I think we should let Megan decide when we're ready to move on."

"Thanks," Megan said. "Ready to go back?"

"Can we rest just another minute?" Carla pleaded.

"Okay, one more minute," Megan relented. She glanced at Carla curiously. She didn't look all that exhausted. "Carla, do you *like* playing tennis?"

"Of course I do," Carla said quickly. "That's why I asked if I could take lessons. I've just *got* to get better."

Megan was startled by the passion in her voice. She suddenly sounded more determined than she had in a week of coaching sessions. And yet, none of that enthusiasm showed up on the court. Megan didn't know what to make of her.

She turned to Leslie. "Why did you want to take lessons?"

Leslie spoke matter-of-factly. "Back home, we have a junior tennis league at our community center. Every year, I get beat in the finals by Wendy Lockwood." The way she practically spat out that name, it was very clear what she thought of this Wendy Lockwood, whoever she was. Her next words confirmed this.

"See, I can't stand Wendy. At school, she beats me in the spelling bee every year. In ballet class, she got the role I wanted in our recital. I've *got* to beat her at *something*."

Megan grimaced. "But do you *like* playing tennis?"

Leslie shrugged. "Yeah, I guess so. It's okay."

"Polly, what about you?" Megan asked. "Why did you want lessons?"

Polly's quick smile made her response almost unnecessary. "I just love tennis, that's all."

At least Megan could understand *one* of her students. "C'mon, then, let's play."

For the next twenty minutes, Megan worked with them, until even *she* was sick of going

11

through the motions of the forehand ground stroke.

"I'm going to serve each of you one more ball," she said. "Then that will be all for today. Carla, you first, then Leslie, then Polly." She ran over to the other side of the court.

It was then that she noticed Ms. Winkle standing just outside the court. There was a man with her, someone Megan had never seen before. Probably a visiting parent getting the camp tour, Megan thought.

She waved to the camp director, and then turned toward the net. For Carla, she decided to use a flat serve. That would be the easiest for Carla to return, and she wanted the sad-faced girl to leave her lesson in a good mood. With her left hand, she tossed the ball up and whipped her racket into it.

The ball curved to the left, just the way Megan wanted it to go. It was headed directly toward Carla. But Carla darted to the right, as if she expected the ball to change direction in mid-air. She barely managed to make contact with it, and it fell lifelessly against the net.

Megan tried not to let her disappointment in Carla show. "Not bad," she called out encouragingly. But Carla's bleak expression made it clear that she didn't buy that.

With Leslie, Megan used the same service, but Leslie's response was much better than Carla's. It wasn't a great return, but she did manage to demonstrate a satisfactory ground stroke.

As Polly took over the position, Megan grinned. Now she could have a little fun. This time, she delivered a different service, making the ball blast down onto the other side of the court in an almost straight line. She was pleased to see that Polly was able to deal with it, slamming it right back.

The girls waved as they ran off the court. "See you tomorrow," Megan called. Then she ran around the court, scooping up the tennis balls. When she finished, she was surprised to see Ms. Winkle and the man still standing there. Ms. Winkle beckoned to her, and Megan joined them. As she drew closer, she realized the man couldn't be a parent. He looked much too young.

"Megan, this is Gary Warren," Ms. Winkle said. "He's a counselor at Camp Eagle."

"How do you do?" Megan said politely, wondering what he was doing here.

Gary Warren didn't exactly have the world's greatest manners. He didn't bother with any "hello" or "pleased to meet you." He wasn't even smiling as he asked Megan, "Where did you learn to play tennis?"

Megan explained how she'd been taking tennis lessons off and on since she was eight, from a friend of her parents' who had been a real tennis champion years ago. She waited for the usual compliments she always received when people had seen her play. But he just gazed at her steadily, his blue eyes cold and critical. "Your toss had too much spin," he said. "And you bent too much at the waist when you went into your swing."

Megan stared at him, dumbfounded. Then he turned abruptly and started walking away.

"Mr. Warren will be our guest at dinner tonight," Ms. Winkle told Megan hurriedly. "And you'll hear about some exciting plans he's got for us."

"What kind of plans?" Megan asked. But Ms. Winkle was already hurrying after him.

With their backs to her, Megan stuck out her tongue at Gary Warren. Maybe they were organizing another intercamp competition between Sunnyside and Eagle. But what was so exciting about that? They had competitions with Eagle all the time. And if Gary Warren was involved in it, Megan wouldn't be interested anyway.

Whatever it was, she'd find out at dinner. Her stomach growled, and she realized she was very hungry. The mysterious Gary Warren faded from her thoughts. She was much more interested in finding out what was for dinner.

Chapter 2

"Hi, guys," Megan called as she entered cabin six. "How was archery?"

The question was greeted by a chorus of groans. Sarah, sitting on her top bunk, responded by taking her pillow and tossing it down on Megan's head.

"You know what I think?" Katie mused. No one bothered to ask what, because they knew they'd hear Katie's idea anyway. "I think we should come up with a new camp activity, something we could propose to Ms. Winkle as a substitute for archery."

"Like what?" Trina asked.

"I don't know," Katie replied. "How about mud wrestling?"

"Very funny," Erin commented. She sat cross-legged on her bed, staring at a finger as if she was hypnotized by it.

Trina laughed. "At least there's one thing you can say in favor of archery. You don't get dirty playing it."

"But every time I string a bow, I break a nail," Erin complained. "Katie, you should think of an activity that won't mess up anything."

"How about a reading period?" Sarah suggested. "I think that would be an excellent camp activity."

"You *would*," Katie teased. "You'd read all day if we didn't shove you out of the cabin."

Megan sighed. "I wish Sunnyside would get a real tennis counselor and we could have tennis as a regular activity."

"You already play tennis practically every day during free period," Katie pointed out. "And now that you're giving these lessons, you've got tennis twice a day."

Megan's eyes sparkled. "But if tennis was on the schedule, like horseback riding, I could play three times a day."

Katie rolled her eyes. "You won't be happy until you're playing nothing *but* tennis."

"With breaks for meals," Megan added. "Hey, I'm hungry. Isn't it time for dinner?"

In answer to her question, the counselor's door opened and Carolyn came out. "Get ready for dinner, girls. We're leaving in five minutes. Megan, how was your tennis group today?"

"Not bad," Megan replied. "One of the girls is really good. But the other two . . ."

"Not so good?" Carolyn asked.

"Well, they're not *terrible*. But it's like they're playing for the wrong reasons. One of them just wants to get good enough so she can beat some girl she doesn't like back home. And the other one keeps saying she has to get better at tennis, but she doesn't act like she's having any fun. What's the point of playing any game if you don't have fun playing it?"

"I don't know," Carolyn said. "Maybe you can have a private talk with her about it." She clapped her hands. "C'mon, girls, hurry up. We don't want to be late tonight."

"What's so special about tonight?" Katie asked.

"Spaghetti and meatballs," Sarah piped up. "I could smell the sauce when I passed the dining hall."

"That's worth hurrying for." Megan started toward the bathroom to wash up.

"I'm sure it is," Carolyn said, "but that wasn't what I was referring to. There's going to

18

be a guest tonight and a special announcement."

Everyone looked up. Erin actually stopped filing her nails for a second.

Megan paused. "Oh, yeah, I heard about that."

Carolyn gave her a slight head shake and put a finger to her lips. "It's supposed to be a secret. I should have known you'd find out before anyone else."

"I don't know what the announcement is," Megan said. "But I met the guest. Gary somebody. He's a counselor at Eagle. What's he doing here, anyway?"

Now Carolyn smiled. "If you don't know, I'm not going to tell you. Let it be a surprise for you too. Girls, I want everyone ready to leave in one minute." She disappeared back into her room.

"Ooh, I love surprises," Sarah said, climbing down from her bunk.

"I wouldn't count on this surprise being a very good one," Megan commented. "Not if that Gary person's got anything to do with it."

"What's the matter with him?" Trina asked.

"He's creepy. He was watching me hit tennis balls to my students. And when I met him, he wasn't nice at all. He criticized my serves!"

Erin gave her fingernail one last swipe. "Maybe you're not as good at tennis as you think you are."

"Erin!" Sarah exclaimed in outrage. "How can you say that? Everyone knows that Megan's the best tennis player at Sunnyside."

"Big deal," Erin snorted. "Sunnyside's just one little camp. Just because Megan's the best here doesn't mean much. If Megan was a really great tennis player, she'd be rich and famous, like, like Steffi Graff or someone like that."

Erin's words didn't bother Megan. She was always putting her cabin mates down in one way or another, and they never took her too seriously. "I don't need to be rich and famous." She grinned. "As long as I can beat everyone at Sunnyside, that's all that matters to me."

Carolyn emerged from her room. "Okay, girls, let's go."

The aroma of spaghetti sauce filled the dining hall, and Megan's mouth began to water in anticipation. The girls collected their trays, and they were just sitting down at their table when Megan saw him. "There's Gary. Over there, with Ms. Winkle."

Erin grabbed Megan's arm. "Megan! You didn't tell us he's gorgeous!"

"Gorgeous? Him?" Megan gazed at him skeptically. Okay, maybe he wasn't ugly, but gorgeous?

To her surprise, everyone else was agreeing. "He looks like a movie star," Katie sighed. "He's better-looking than Darrell, even."

The girls automatically put their hands over their hearts, the way they always did when the swimming coach's name was mentioned. But their eyes were still on the Eagle counselor.

Ms. Winkle went to the front of the room. "Girls, may I have your attention? I have a very exciting announcement to make."

The noise level in the room dropped slightly, and some faces turned toward the front. Ms. Winkle was clutching a card in her hand, her hair was wilder than usual, and her face was flushed. Megan realized this was going to be something a lot bigger than another softball game with Camp Eagle.

"I am thrilled to report that Camp Sunnyside has been selected for a very great honor." She paused dramatically. Now the room fell silent, and the campers' expressions became expectant.

As soon as she knew she had everyone's full attention, Ms. Winkle spoke again, reading from the card in her hand. "We will be hosting the

21

very first annual Girls' Summer Camp Invitational Tournament!"

"A tournament for what?" someone called out.

Ms. Winkle blinked. Then she looked at the card again and tittered. "Sorry, I left out a word. It's the Girls' Summer Camp Invitational *Tennis* Tournament!"

Megan gasped, and clapped a hand to her mouth. "A tennis tournament?" she breathed. "Here?"

"In just a week," Ms. Winkle continued, "camps all over the state will be sending their best tennis players here to Sunnyside to compete."

Megan could feel the hairs standing up on her arms. None of the other girls at her table looked particularly thrilled, since none of them was into tennis. But this was the most awesome event ever to happen at Sunnyside as far as Megan was concerned.

"Not only is it an honor to host the tournament," Ms. Winkle continued, "we, that is, Camp Sunnyside, will also be getting a lot of publicity. We may have representatives from newspapers, magazines, and possibly even television here."

With that information, a buzz went through the room. Megan's head was spinning. Still, she wondered what Gary Warren had to do with this.

From the back of the dining hall, a shrill voice called out. "Ms. Winkle?"

The camp director peered out at the crowd. "Yes?"

"Yuck," Katie muttered in an undertone. "It's Maura Kingsley."

Megan turned to see the meanest girl at Camp Sunnyside stand up. "How will you choose the Sunnyside girls who are going to compete in the tournament?" Maura asked.

Ms. Winkle laughed lightly. "Well, *I* won't be choosing them. I'm no judge of tennis. And since we don't have a tennis specialist here, we've borrowed one. I'd like to introduce you all to Gary Warren, from Camp Eagle."

"Are we supposed to applaud?" Sarah asked in a whisper.

"I'd clap for him any day," Erin murmured.

Megan barely heard them. She was staring at Gary Warren. So that's why he had the nerve to criticize her tennis. She remembered Stewart, her friend from Eagle, mentioning their tennis instructor, Gary. She hadn't connected

23

the names. And she had no memory of what Stewart had actually said about him.

She realized that all her cabin mates, even sensible Trina, were gazing dreamily at the Eagle counselor. And then she noticed that practically every girl in the dining hall over the age of nine was looking at him the same way.

Personally, Megan couldn't understand it. The guy didn't even smile as he addressed the group.

"I'll be selecting the Sunnyside girls who will compete in the tournament. I'm hoping to find four suitable players. And once I've selected them, I'll be working very closely with those girls all this week to get them ready for next week's competition. Those of you who are interested in trying out, meet with me tomorrow at ten A.M. on the tennis court." He started to walk away, and then he looked back. "And keep in mind, if you are interested, that serious competition demands sacrifice."

"Sacrifice," Megan repeated. "I wonder what that's supposed to mean?"

"Probably that you're going to have to work very, very hard," Carolyn said. "And you may have to give up some other activities you like doing."

24

Trina nodded in agreement. "If you're having the tryouts at ten o'clock tomorrow morning, you'll have to give up horseback riding."

Megan grimaced slightly. Next to tennis, riding horses was her favorite activity. Why couldn't he have scheduled the tryouts during rest period?

"Big deal—you can ride horses any day," Katie said. "Megan, aren't you excited? I thought you'd be jumping up and down by now."

Megan's *stomach* was jumping up and down. She was still feeling a little dazed. "Of course I'm excited! It's just that, well, I've never played in a tournament before."

"Then this is a great opportunity for you," Carolyn noted. "Your very first real tennis competition."

"And you heard what Ms. Winkle said," Erin remarked. "There will be people from newspapers and television here. Megan, if you win this tournament, you could become a professional!"

"Wow," Sarah murmured. "Just think about it! You'll be traveling all over the world, playing in all those tournaments that are on TV."

Trina smiled warmly at Megan. "Are you going to remember us when you're rich and famous?"

25

Katie speared a meatball. "Yeah, maybe we should get her autograph now before she forgets who we are."

"Now, girls, let's not get carried away," Carolyn cautioned them. "You're going to make Megan nervous."

"That's okay," Megan assured her. "I never get nervous about playing tennis. Besides, I have to get picked in the tryouts tomorrow before I can even be in the tournament."

"Come on, you know you'll get chosen to play," Sarah said.

Megan didn't even blush as she nodded. She knew there was no point in faking modesty with these kids.

Erin was twirling her fork slowly through the spaghetti, and staring off into space. "I know *I'd* be nervous."

"Of course you'd be," Katie said. "You can barely play tennis at all."

"I'm not talking about tennis," Erin said. "I'm talking about *him.*"

"Gary Warren?" Megan asked.

"Who else? Remember, he said he'd be working closely all week with the girls he picked. Oh, Megan, you're so lucky!"

Megan took a furtive glance toward the table

where the Eagle counselor was eating with Ms. Winkle. Maybe he was nicer than he'd appeared to be so far. If she was going to have to work with him, she certainly hoped so.

"I wonder who else is going to try out for the tournament," Megan said as they were leaving the dining hall.

"Let's go over to the activities hall," Katie suggested. "Maybe we'll find out there."

Since there weren't any special activities going on at camp that evening, the activities hall was crowded and lively. The cabin six girls headed for the room where the Ping-Pong tables were, but all the tables were occupied.

And occupying one side of a table was Maura Kingsley. The thirteen year old was playing one of her cabin nine friends. Other girls from cabin nine stood around the table.

The cabin six girls stood there, watching her with generally grim expressions. If they had one real enemy at Sunnyside, it was Maura Kingsley. Megan couldn't begin to count up the number of nasty things Maura had done to them. There was the color war, when she had been captain of one side and poor Trina had been on her team. Maura had almost driven Trina crazy. And then there was the time Erin was hanging

27

out at cabin nine. Maura had tried to get her to do things that almost got Erin into serious trouble.

Megan watched as Maura whacked the Ping-Pong ball so hard it practically hit her opponent in the face.

"Maura, be careful!" her friend exclaimed.

Maura didn't apologize, and her laugh wasn't at all regretful. "I keep forgetting this is Ping-Pong," she said. "I've got my mind on tennis."

"Are you trying to try out for the tournament?" one of her friends asked.

"Of course," Maura replied.

"I've never seen her playing tennis," Katie whispered to Megan.

"I did, once," Megan replied in an undertone.

"Is she any good?"

Megan shrugged. "So-so."

Just then, Maura spotted them watching her. She handed her Ping-Pong paddle over to another cabin nine girl, and sauntered over to them.

"Hello, Megan," she drawled in a suspiciously sweet manner. "I was just wondering if you're planning to try out for the tennis tournament tomorrow."

"I was thinking about it," Megan said casually.

Maura's eyebrows shot up, as if she was astonished by this reply. "Really? I didn't think you'd have the nerve."

"Why not?" Katie moved in front of Megan and faced Maura squarely. "You know Megan's the best tennis player here."

Maura's face was all innocence. "I just didn't think she'd enjoy playing in front of a crowd, with everyone watching every move she makes."

Megan involuntarily shuddered. She hadn't even thought about that. Would having an audience make a difference in the way she played?

"You're just trying to freak her out," Katie said in disgust. "You're afraid if she tries out, you won't get picked."

Maura tossed back her head and laughed, as if Katie's comment was totally absurd. Then her eyes took on an all-too-familiar meanness. "For your information, I play quite a bit of tennis back home. And *I've* competed in tournaments." With that comment, she shot Megan a triumphant smile, whirled around, and went back to her friends.

Sarah sidled up next to Megan. "Don't let her bother you. You know what she's like."

"I know," Megan said. She bit her lip. "But I never thought about people *watching* me play tennis. Remember when we put on that play for the Sunnyside Spectacular? I had so much stage fright, I practically forgot all my lines!"

"Don't be ridiculous," Katie said briskly. "Playing tennis is nothing like being in a play. Besides, Megan, you're an excellent tennis player. But you're a *terrible* actress!"

Megan couldn't help laughing. Katie was absolutely right. "I hope some other kids are trying out who are better than Maura," she said. "I hate the idea of practicing with her all week." Her eyes roamed the room, searching for likely candidates. Then she spotted one. "I'll be right back," she told her cabin mates. She headed toward the group of younger kids.

"Polly!" she called.

The nine year old came over. "Hi, Megan! Isn't that exciting about the tennis tournament?" Polly asked. "I guess you'll be playing in it."

"I'm definitely going to try out," Megan replied. "What about you?"

30

"Me?" Polly's voice rose to a squeak. "You think I should try out for the tournament?"

"Sure," Megan said. "Why not?"

Polly's eyes were the size of saucers. "But—but do you think I'm good enough?"

"You've been doing really well," Megan told her. "I'll bet you're better than most girls here at Sunnyside."

Polly hugged herself and hopped up and down. "Do you honestly think that counselor will pick me?"

"I have no idea," Megan replied honestly. "And I hope you won't be too disappointed if he doesn't choose you. But it's worth a try."

Her two other students joined them. Polly turned to them excitedly. "Megan thinks I should try out for the tennis tournament!"

Megan looked at Leslie and Carla anxiously. She hoped they wouldn't be jealous.

But Carla just seemed happy for Polly. "That's great," she said. "Leslie, are you going to try out?"

Leslie shook her head vehemently. "No way. I've heard too much about Gary Warren."

"What do you know about him?" Megan asked.

"My brother goes to Camp Eagle," Leslie ex-

31

plained. "He quit playing tennis because of him. He says Gary Warren is a real slave driver, and he yells all the time, and he never lets you take a break."

Something clicked in Megan's head. Then she remembered. *Slave driver.* Those were almost exactly the same words Stewart had used when he mentioned Gary Warren.

"Really?" Polly sounded worried.

Leslie nodded solemnly. "So if you get picked to be in the tournament, you better get ready to work till you drop dead of exhaustion."

Now Polly looked frightened. "Stop that," Megan scolded Leslie. "You're exaggerating. He couldn't be that bad."

"I hope not," Polly said.

"Besides, how could he work us to death?" Megan asked. "We'll be playing tennis." She draped a comforting arm around Polly. "I wouldn't call tennis work, would you?"

Polly shook her head. "No."

Megan grinned. "Well, we're certainly not going to drop dead from having too much fun!"

Chapter 3

At a few minutes before ten o'clock the next morning, Megan walked along the path to the tennis court with Sarah. "Thanks for giving up horseback riding to come with me," Megan said. "I feel I need a friend."

"No problem," Sarah said cheerfully. "I don't mind. The horses are probably happy to have a break from *me*."

Megan giggled. It was true that whenever Sarah got on a horse, she clamped her feet into the poor animal and clung to the reins for dear life.

"But I don't understand why you wanted me to come with you," Sarah continued. "You're such a great tennis player, there's no way you won't get chosen. Why are you so nervous?"

Megan's hand tightened on the racket she clutched under her arm. "Oh, I'm not nervous,"

Megan assured her. "It's just that—I don't know—I just feel a little weird about trying out for a tournament."

"Why?"

"I don't know," Megan said again. She really didn't. Tennis never made her feel jumpy like this. Tennis was fun! Playing it, even just thinking about it, always made her happy. If she got chosen, there would be practices all week, and the tournament next week. She'd be playing more tennis than she ever usually got to play at Sunnyside. What could be finer than that?

"You know," Sarah said, "I've heard of special tennis camps, where that's all the campers do—play tennis. How come you don't go to one of those?"

"Because I'm perfectly happy at Sunnyside," Megan said promptly. "My parents asked me if I wanted to go to one of those tennis camps this year, and I said no. I'd miss all the other stuff we do, like the horses and the arts and crafts and canoeing. And I'd miss you guys." She pretended to swat Sarah with her racket. "Hey, do you want to get rid of me?"

Sarah laughed. "No way. Hey, it's almost ten. We'd better hurry." The girls linked arms and ran the rest of the way. It's great having a best friend, Megan thought happily. Already, she was feeling less and less nervous.

But when they arrived at the court, her stomach started hopping again. There were at least fifteen girls gathered on the benches just outside the court. Some were sitting stiffly, with tense faces. Others were giggling nervously. Megan and Sarah found spaces at the end of one bench and sat down.

"Hi, Megan."

Megan looked up to see Carla approaching them. She was smiling, but it was a strange sort of smile, like she was forcing it.

"Hi, Carla." She introduced her to Sarah. "Are you here to watch?"

Carla shook her head and then swallowed. "No, I'm . . . I'm trying out."

Megan tried not to let her astonishment show, but it was impossible. "You are? You didn't say anything about trying out last night."

"I—I didn't think I was going to. But I got a letter from my father this morning. And I changed my mind."

How could a letter from her father change her mind? Megan wondered. He couldn't have known about the tournament. *They* only learned about it yesterday.

35

Carla was twisting her hands. Her face was pale, her eyes wide and frightened, and she looked like someone who was about to be sick. Megan knew that even in the best of health, Carla wasn't anywhere near good enough to be in a tennis tournament. But she couldn't bring herself to say anything. The girl looked scared enough already.

"Well, good luck," Megan said lamely.

The quivering smile appeared again on Carla's face. Then she hurried away to another bench.

"She looks like this is the last place in the world she wants to be," Sarah said. "What's her problem?"

"I'm not sure," Megan said thoughtfully. "But I'm going to find out."

Sarah made a face. "*There's* someone who doesn't look nervous," she noted.

Maura was walking by, accompanied on each side by two of her friends. Her head was high, and she carried an air of extreme confidence. Megan tried to recall exactly how well Maura could play from the one time she watched her. Was she really better than Megan remembered?

"Check her out," Sarah whispered. "The queen with her ladies-in-waiting. Like she's

36

somebody special, when everyone knows the truth."

Megan couldn't help grinning. Maura always did pretend she was better than anyone else at everything. And she never was. She needed Sarah to give her that little reminder. Now she was doubly glad she'd asked Sarah to come and keep her company today. Her spirits soared even higher when she saw Polly waving. She beckoned her over.

"I'm so excited!" Polly bubbled. "Keep your fingers crossed for me, okay?"

Megan obligingly held up crossed fingers. "And you keep yours crossed for me!"

Polly giggled, and hooked one finger over another. "I'll do it, but *you* don't need any luck! Ooh, here comes that counselor." She ran back to where she'd been sitting.

Megan tried to look at Gary Warren objectively. In all fairness, she had to admit he was handsome, with his sun-streaked brown hair and clear blue eyes. He wore traditional tennis clothes, white shorts and a white shirt that made his golden tan look even darker. But he still wasn't smiling. In fact, his lips were set in a firm line. The words *slave driver* kept popping into Megan's head.

He stood before the girls and his eyes surveyed the group. There were no words of greeting, no welcome speech, no pep talk. "Is there anyone here who is not planning to try out for the tournament?"

Several girls, including Maura's two companions and Sarah, raised their hands.

"You're going to have to leave," he said. "This is serious business, and I don't want any spectators making any noise or cheering their friends."

One girl started to protest. The only words she got out were "But I want my friend—" before a cold look from Gary Warren silenced her.

"Sorry," Sarah whispered. She gave Megan's hand a quick squeeze. "Good luck."

Megan managed a smile before Sarah hurried away. As soon as the friends and supporters had left the area, the counselor spoke again. "As you probably know, I'm Gary Warren, tennis coach from Camp Eagle. I will be selecting the tournament participants. But first—"

"Excuse me!"

It was obvious that Gary Warren did not like to be interrupted. The face he turned toward Maura was grim. "What do you want?" he snapped.

His tone didn't seem to bother Maura. She gave him a flirtatious smile. "What would you like us to call you? Mr. Warren or Gary?"

"Neither. You can call me Coach. And don't interrupt me again."

Maura actually looked startled. She wasn't used to being spoken to like that.

"I'm passing out cards," he continued. "Write down your name, age, and cabin number." He walked down the row of girls, handing each a card. "When you're done, I'll pair you off. You won't be playing a full set, just enough so I can see what you can do. The names of the girls who will participate in the tournament will be posted on the dining hall at noon."

On her card, Megan carefully printed "Megan Lindsay, age 11, cabin 6." As Coach Warren went back down the row collecting the cards, he asked, "Have any of you ever participated in a tennis tournament before?"

Maura's hand shot up.

"Where?" he asked.

Maura preened. "I won the tournament for thirteen year olds at my country club last fall."

Coach Warren dismissed that with a wave of his hand. "No, no, I'm talking about *real* tournaments." He ignored Maura's crestfallen face, and studied the row. "You and you." Two girls of approximately the same size rose uncertainly. "What are your names?" When they stammered them out, he pulled their cards. "Let's see what you can do." He pointed to one girl. "You can serve."

Both girls moved awkwardly onto the court. The server tossed the ball, and missed it. "I'm sorry," she called out.

"Just do it again," Coach Warren barked.

Megan watched as the girl managed to serve the second ball. The two girls volleyed weakly for about a minute before Coach Warren blew his whistle. "That's enough. You two can go." The players shook hands and left the court.

Coach Warren glanced at the line, and pointed. "You. And you."

The second pair played even worse than the first pair had. Megan felt sorry for them, but her own sense of confidence began to grow.

The next two chosen to play were Polly and Carla. They might have been exactly the same size, but it wasn't exactly an even match. From the first moment they started playing, all of Carla's problems were clearly evident—the way she froze before running to meet a ball, her poor stance, and the lack of power behind her strokes.

It was painful to watch her, so Megan concentrated on Polly.

Polly was super. Megan beamed with pride as she watched her star student whiz around the court, looking far more experienced than she really was. Her eyes darted back and forth between the talented player and Coach Warren, hoping she'd see something like approval on his face. Surely he must see how good she is, Megan thought. But you'd never know from his expression. It remained a blank.

Still, Megan felt sure that Polly had to be impressing him. She was the best so far. When he blew his whistle, she waited to see if he'd compliment her. He didn't.

The girls shook hands and came off the court. Megan was afraid Carla would come by and want to know how she did. She didn't think she'd be able to lie very easily. She was almost relieved when Carla hurried away and started toward the path leading to the cabins.

Polly caught Megan's eye, and Megan gave her a thumbs-up sign. She motioned for Polly to come over to her.

"You did great!" she said.

Before Polly could reply, Coach Warren blew

his whistle. "Quiet!" he shouted. Then he pointed directly at Megan. "You. And . . . you."

Polly flashed crossed fingers at Megan and ran off. Megan stood up and looked to see who Coach Warren had selected as her opponent.

For a moment, her heart sank. Maura stood there, gazing at Megan with her cockiest expression. But she's at least four inches taller than me, Megan wanted to protest. Then she realized that *all* the girls who were left were taller than she was.

"C'mon, get moving!" the coach yelled. "We don't have all day!"

Megan clutched her racket and followed Maura out onto the court. As she got into position, she clenched her teeth. An image formed in her head—Maura, making fun of Sarah in the swimming pool. Maybe this was for the best. At least she'd be playing someone she really wanted to beat. She only hoped her strong feelings wouldn't mess up her form.

Maura had the serve, and she executed a pretty decent one. Megan returned it neatly. But after a couple of volleys, she realized that Maura was only a so-so player. She could return a ball if it landed where she expected it to land, but she couldn't handle surprises.

42

So Megan started hitting her with strong attacking shots, fast, deep, and designed to force Maura to make errors. She was so deep in concentration that she jumped when she heard the coach's whistle.

Out of breath, Megan hurried over to the side of the court and stuck out her right hand to shake Maura's. Maura gazed at Megan's sweaty palm in disgust. "It's not a real game. We don't have to shake."

Megan shrugged. "Nice game," she lied, smiling sweetly. Maura flounced off. Megan turned to Coach Warren, and her smile faded. He didn't even glance at her as he picked the next two players.

Megan wanted to stick around and see how the other girls did. But as she started to take a seat on the bench, Coach Warren actually turned to her. "You can leave now."

But even his cold voice couldn't bring her down. She'd played as well as she could, and she knew it. She felt as high as a kite, and she ran off to find her cabin mates.

They were all just leaving the stables when Megan arrived. "Did you get chosen?" Sarah asked eagerly.

"Won't know till noon," Megan said breath-

43

lessly. "You're not going to believe who I had to play!" She didn't give them time to guess. "Maura!"

"I hope you blew her off the court," Katie said.

Megan didn't bother to be humble. "You better believe it! What time is it?"

Trina checked her watch. "Almost eleven."

Megan groaned. "How am I going to wait a whole hour till the names are posted?"

"Well, it's free period," Erin said. She eyed Megan's sweaty tee shirt in distaste. "You could go back to the cabin and take a shower."

"I've got a better idea," Katie said. "Let's go over to arts and crafts and work on the mural."

Megan agreed. She doubted that would take her mind off things, but it was better than doing nothing. And there was something special she did want to add to the mural.

There weren't too many kids in the arts and crafts cabin. Megan grabbed some markers and went to the space where the tennis court would be. "Darn!" she exclaimed. "Somebody already drew the court."

Sarah came over to look. "Well, at least whoever it was did a nice job."

Megan had to agree. The court was drawn

44

neatly, with nice straight lines, and someone had taken a lot of time to make the net, with perfectly even crisscross lines.

"But there are no players yet," Sarah pointed out.

Megan had noticed that too. And with a smile, she got to work. "Trina," she called, "could you outline two people for me? On each side of the court?"

Trina was the best at drawing figures. But once she'd done the basic outline, Megan took over. When she finished, she called the others over. "Who does that look like?"

Katie studied the picture. "Hmm . . . curly red hair, freckles, blue eyes . . . I can't imagine who that's supposed to be."

"Hey, that's cool!" Sarah said. "We should each paint ourselves on the mural, in the places where we like to be most. Me in the cabin reading, Katie on a horse, Trina on the diving board, and—hey, Erin, where do you want to be?"

Katie answered for her. "In front of a mirror."

"Very funny," Erin said. She peered down at Megan's drawing. "Hey, that could be what's her name, that little girl who takes your tennis lessons."

Megan looked at the figure. Erin was right. Polly had red hair and freckles too. "Oh, well," she said contentedly, "I know it's me. And that's what counts."

"Who are you going to make your opponent look like?" Sarah asked.

"I'm going to wait till the tournament starts," Megan replied. "And I'll put the girl who's the best player on the other side." Then she struck a pose. "I mean, the *second-best* player!"

Erin raised her eyebrows. "You sound pretty sure of yourself."

Megan flushed. But she couldn't help it. She just knew she'd get picked. Still, she wished the hour would pass quickly so she could find out for sure.

She busied herself working with Sarah on the forest. She worked on making little spots of green for leaves. While she dotted the mural, her mind conjured up images of the tournament. She could see herself, swooping across the court, and she could hear the resounding whack of the ball against her racket. Crowds cheered, and scores rang in her ears—"Six—love, Lindsay! Six—love, Lindsay!" Her opponents gazed at her with envy and admiration.

With a great deal of effort, she tried to envision Coach Warren congratulating her, patting her on the back, shaking her hand, smiling. But even her wild imagination couldn't come up with that image.

"It's twelve o'clock!" Trina called out.

It was as if her mind now became a television screen that had just been turned off. Megan froze. "Come on!" Sarah yelled, grabbing her hand. Megan allowed herself to be dragged away.

What if she was wrong? she thought frantically as they all raced toward the dining hall. What if she hadn't been as good as she thought she'd been?

Running up to the bulletin board by the side of the dining hall door, she could see a white sheet posted. As she got closer, she saw the big letters on top of the sheet: Sunnyside Tournament Players. Then she was face-to-face with four typed names.

And one of them was Megan Lindsay.

A whoop went up from her cabin mates. Everyone, even Erin, was hugging Megan. "You're going to be a star!" Sarah shrieked.

"We should put a banner on our cabin," Katie shouted gleefully. " 'Megan Lindsay lives here!' "

47

"Megan, we're so proud of you," Trina added warmly.

"Maybe they'll put her on television and we can all be there with her," Erin suggested.

"Hold on, you guys." Megan laughed. "I'm just *in* the tournament. I haven't won it." It dawned on her that she hadn't even checked the other names yet. When she did, she let out a cry of pleasure. "Polly made it too!"

The other two names were girls Megan barely knew, from cabin eight. "At least Maura didn't make it," Megan said thankfully. The thought of having to spend a week practicing with *her* wasn't exactly a pleasant notion.

"Speak of the devil," Katie muttered. Megan turned. There was Maura, right behind them. And it was clear that she'd heard what Megan had said.

Maura's upper lip curled. "You might be interested in knowing that I asked to have my name withdrawn from consideration."

Megan doubted that very much. But she figured Maura was just embarrassed at not having made it, so she pretended to believe her. "Why did you do that?" she asked politely.

"Because I wouldn't want to work with that awful Gary Warren," Maura replied. "He's nasty and mean. I guess I'm supposed to congratulate you, but actually, I think I should offer my sympathies. I feel sorry for anyone who has to spend time with him."

"Sure you do," Katie sneered.

Erin gazed at Maura in disbelief. "Maura, how can you say that about him? He's so handsome!"

Maura gazed back at her coolly. "You shouldn't judge a book by its cover." Her eyes drifted back to Megan, and she shook her head sadly. Then she walked away.

"She's just jealous," Trina said comfortingly. "He couldn't be that bad."

"Of course he isn't," Megan said staunchly. "I mean, he's not exactly friendly, but I think he's just trying to be tough so we'll all take this seriously. And a good tennis coach *should* be tough." Then she saw someone else coming toward the dining hall. "Uh-oh, it's Carla. Guys, why don't you go on inside and I'll meet you? I think I should talk to her alone."

Her cabin mates went into the dining hall, and Megan waited for Carla. From Carla's woebegone expression, Megan guessed that she'd already seen the list. But when Carla joined her, her first words were, "I didn't make it, did I?"

Megan smiled kindly and put an arm around her. "Don't feel bad. Lots of girls didn't make it. You're just not ready for a tournament yet."

"I don't think I ever will be," Carla said. "I'm never going to be a great tennis player."

"You don't have to be great to enjoy playing the game," Megan said.

She was startled to see tears well up in Carla's eyes. "But I don't even enjoy playing tennis," she blurted out.

Megan could have guessed that from the way Carla acted. But she still didn't understand. "Then why do you play it?"

"My father used to be a professional tennis player," Carla told her. "My older brother plays for his college team, and even my younger sister plays really well."

"So what?" Megan asked. "Just because they're tennis players doesn't mean you have to be one too."

"You don't understand," Carla said. "My father expects us all to play well. Remember, I told you I had a letter from him this morning?" She pulled a crumpled sheet of paper out of her pocket, and read from it. " 'I hope you're working hard on your tennis game. I'm glad to hear that you're getting some special coaching from another camper. I'll be expecting some real improvement when you come home.' "

Megan sighed. "Carla, have you ever tried telling him that you just don't like tennis?"

"I couldn't do that!" Carla exclaimed, looking shocked. "He'd be so disappointed in me. I *have* to get better. You'll still help me, won't you? Even if you have to practice for the tournament?"

"Sure I will," Megan assured her. Carla gave her a small, grateful smile, and went on into the dining hall.

Megan gazed after her with regret. How awful to have to play a game you hated, she thought. As far as she was concerned there was only one good reason to play tennis—for fun.

Gary Warren's stern, grim face passed through her mind. With a firm shake of her head, she pushed it out. Nobody could keep tennis from being fun for her.

Chapter 4

One week later, Megan wasn't having any fun at all. On the other side of the tennis court, Polly hit the ball too hard. From the angle it came over the net, Megan knew it would go out, beyond the boundaries on Megan's side. So she stood there and watched it fly by.

Coach Warren's whistle shrieked across the court. "Lindsay! What's the matter with you? Why are you just standing there?"

Megan flinched. She hated to be yelled at. "It was going out of bounds!" she responded. "What's the point of chasing after a ball that's going out?"

"It was on the line," Coach Warren stated. "It wasn't out. You would have lost a point. Don't ever assume a ball's going out!"

"Yeah, yeah," Megan muttered. She'd been listening to lectures like that all week, and she

52

felt like she was ready to scream. Across the court, Polly was staring off in the opposite direction, politely pretending she couldn't hear Megan getting yelled at.

"It's your serve," the coach barked. "Get the ball."

Megan dragged her feet as she went to the edge of the court. The hot sun beat down on her head, and she pushed damp curls off her forehead. This was supposed to be free period, she thought glumly. And she felt like she was in tennis prison.

Right this very moment, all her cabin mates were probably having a great time in the cool, refreshing swimming pool. She should be in the water with them, jumping off the side in a cannonball, splashing them, and getting dunked. When was the last time she'd been in the pool?

"Lindsay! Move it!"

Megan seethed. That was something else that got on her nerves. Being called by her last name. It sounded so harsh. Strange, when he called Polly "Jackson" it didn't sound so bad. And Polly didn't seem to mind as much.

She snatched up the ball and went to the serving position behind the baseline. She tossed the ball, but as she looked up, the sun hit her right

53

in the eyes, setting off a glare that practically blinded her. She swung the racket wildly and didn't make contact.

She knew she'd hear that shrill whistle, but when it came she jumped anyway. Before Coach Warren could speak, she turned to him. "I couldn't see! The sun got in my eyes!"

"Then you shouldn't have attempted to hit it," he yelled back. "It wouldn't count against you if you didn't swing."

"I know that," Megan responded. "But—"

"I don't want to hear any of your excuses! Serve the ball!"

Once again, Megan tossed the ball. But before she could even begin her swing, the whistle blew again. She caught the ball and turned her head. "Now what?"

Coach Warren ran a hand through his hair, looking as if he was about to tear it out from frustration. "Your foot's on the baseline!"

Megan looked down. He was right.

"That's a double fault," he accused her. "You've blown two serves, and you would have lost a point if this was an actual game."

"But it's not a real game," Megan protested.

"Yeah, well, tomorrow it will be. And if you

play tomorrow the way you're playing right now, you'll be eliminated in the first round."

Polly appeared by his side. "Excuse me, Coach," she said softly. "Could I get some water?"

At least now he had someone else to direct his bad temper on. "What if this was a real game?" he challenged Polly. "You know the rules. You can't take a break until after the second set."

"Okay," she whispered.

He groaned. "All right, I guess that's enough for now."

It should be, Megan thought. They'd been out here for almost three hours!

"But I want to go over some things with you," he added. Behind his back, the girls rolled eyes at each other. But they followed him to a bench.

"Jackson, you're rushing the net," he said. "Watch out for that. And Lindsay, you're showing off again."

Megan gaped in indignation. "What do you mean?"

"I saw you try that deep volley. An angle shot would have been better."

Megan couldn't believe her ears. He was acting like she was some kind of beginner! She'd better let him know she knew what she was do-

55

ing. Keeping her voice even, she said, "I was playing a net game, and a deep volley is good strategy for a net game."

He wasn't impressed. "Well, you shouldn't be playing a net game. Stick with ground strokes. Your volleys are generally weak."

Megan's face was burning. How could he talk to her like that? And in front of Polly! It was incredibly embarrassing to be criticized in front of someone who was younger.

Like a final slap in the face, he added, "And your backhand's getting sloppy."

Through clenched teeth, Megan muttered, "Sorry."

"I don't want apologies," Coach Warren snapped. "I want improvement."

Megan caught a quick glimpse of sympathy in Polly's face. It didn't make her feel better. In fact, it was humiliating to get sympathy from someone who had been her student.

"I want you back here to work on your backhand after dinner," he said.

Megan gasped. "After dinner? But my cabin is taking canoes out after dinner!"

His eyes took on that cold, mean glare she'd learned to dread. "Lindsay, I don't care about your canoes. You're playing in a tennis tournament tomorrow. That's all that should matter to you right now."

Megan was speechless. She knew that, even without words, her dismay had to be written all over her face. But did Coach Warren care? Forget it.

Having just destroyed what was left of Megan's day, he was now giving his attention to Polly, going over each error *she* had made. Megan grabbed her racket and stalked off. Just outside the court, she found herself face-to-face with Carla and Leslie. They were both looking at her in anticipation.

"What do *you* want?" Megan cried out in frustration.

They were both gaping at her with shocked expressions. She'd never used a tone like that with them before. Even as she spoke, she thought she was beginning to sound like Coach Warren.

"Aren't we having our lesson today?" Leslie asked.

Megan shook her head vehemently. "If I have to look at one more tennis ball I'm going to scream!" She was afraid if she stood there one more minute, she really would. She brushed past the girls and headed for the path.

She felt crummy, finking out on her students like that. But she couldn't bear the idea of staying on that court any longer. She'd given up so much that week—all her free periods, not to mention horseback riding, swimming, arts and crafts. All day she'd been looking forward to taking canoes out onto the lake tonight. And now the slave driver was telling her she'd have to give that up too! What was left for her to give up—eating?

She couldn't even share all her bad feelings with anyone. She was too proud to let her cabin mates know how she was suffering. She hardly ever saw them anyway, except at meals.

"Megan!"

She turned and saw Leslie, Carla, and Polly running toward her. "Are you okay?" Polly asked. "Carla said you were upset."

Megan forced a smile. "Sure, I'm fine. I'm sorry I talked to you guys like that. I guess I'm just in a bad mood."

"How come?" Polly asked.

"You heard the way Coach Warren was criticizing me."

"He just wants you to be your best tomorrow," Polly said.

Megan's eyes widened. Was she defending him?

"I know he's not very friendly," Polly continued, "but he's a good coach."

Megan scratched her head. "I'm glad *you* think so." She turned and started away, but Carla touched her arm. "Megan . . ."

"What?"

"You don't sound like you're having much fun."

"Huh?"

"You said the only reason to play tennis is to have fun. Are you having fun?"

Megan sighed. She had no answer for that.

"Megan, how come you're so quiet?" Katie asked at dinner.

"She's probably daydreaming about the tournament tomorrow," Erin said.

"Are you nervous?" Carolyn asked.

Megan hesitated. She never thought tennis would ever make her feel nervous. But she didn't exactly feel cool and calm. "Maybe a little," she admitted.

Carolyn gazed at her in concern. "Would it help to talk about it?"

"Yeah," Trina said, "why don't you tell us

59

what it's going to be like? I've never been to a real tennis tournament before."

Neither had Megan, but she'd seen tournaments on TV. "Tomorrow will be the first round of play, and the next day there's the second round."

"Do you know who you'll be playing?" Sarah asked.

"No, I won't know till after the draw tomorrow morning. Each player's name is on a card, and then the cards are drawn out one at a time. Each name is put on a chart in the order that it's drawn. So in the first round, the first player plays the second one, the third plays the fourth, and so on."

"What happens if you lose in the first round?" Katie asked. "Do you get to try again in the second round?"

"No. It's a single elimination tournament. As soon as you lose one match, you're out."

Sarah shivered. "No second chances, huh?"

Megan shook her head. "After the two rounds, there will only be eight people left. They play in the quarter finals. The four who win those play in the semi-finals. The last two left play the final match."

Katie beamed at her. "And one of them will be you, right?"

One week ago, Megan might have agreed. Now she wasn't so sure. She got up. "I'm going back to the cabin."

"But you haven't had dessert yet," Sarah pointed out.

"I'm not that hungry. And I have to go back to the court in a little while for more practice."

Trina looked at her in surprise. "Aren't you going out in the canoes with us?"

Megan didn't trust herself to speak. She just shook her head and started toward the door. She had reached it when Sarah caught up with her.

"Megan, you never pass up dessert. And you've been quiet all week. What's wrong?"

Megan couldn't keep up a brave front with Sarah. She kept walking, but as soon as they emerged from the dining hall, she let it all out.

"Oh, Sarah, it's been awful! He's horrible! Honestly, he's the meanest man in the world!"

Sarah was bewildered. "Who are you talking about?"

"That coach! Gary Warren! As far as he's concerned, everything I do is wrong. He yells at me all the time, more than he yells at any of the others. Either he just doesn't like me, or—or . . ."

61

And now she was on the verge of tears. "Or I'm just not a very good tennis player."

"That's crazy!" Sarah exclaimed. "Why, you're the best tennis player I've ever seen!"

That brought a small smile to Megan's face. "How many have you seen?"

"Not that many," Sarah admitted. "Actually, none. But Megan, don't *you* think you're good?"

"Yeah. At least, I did. Up till now."

"Then you are! And you know what you have to do tomorrow?"

"What?"

"Prove that you're right and he's wrong! Get out there on the court and show him how good you really are."

"But what if I have a really tough opponent?"

"Then you'll be tougher! Look, I don't know what's the matter with this guy. Maybe he just needs someone to pick on, and he picked you. But that's not important. You know you can play tennis. And when you beat that poor girl, whoever she is, tomorrow, he'll know it too!"

Megan was silent for a minute. Then she said, "Gee, Sarah, I never knew you were so good at giving pep talks."

"Am I?"

"Well, I feel better. In fact, I feel a lot better."

She could feel a spark of her old confidence growing inside her. "You know, Sarah, you're right. I'm going to show that guy exactly how wrong he is about me. I'm going to get out there tomorrow and wipe that girl off the court!"

"That's the spirit," Sarah cried out. "Wow, I don't even know the girl and I already feel sorry for her!"

The spark of confidence burst into a flame. Megan gave her buddy a grateful hug. Then she marched off toward the court, hoping the flame would still be burning tomorrow.

Chapter 5

The flame of confidence wasn't exactly raging the next morning as Megan set off for the tennis court. But there was still a flicker glowing inside, and Megan hoped it would turn into a real fire by the time of her match.

Her thoughts went back to her practice session the evening before. Once again, Coach Warren had yelled and scolded and made her hit the same strokes over and over. But she pushed that memory away. If today's match went the way she thought it could, he'd be treating her a lot differently from now on.

Just as she was passing cabin four, Polly came out. The younger redhead was so pale, her freckles stood out like measles. Remembering how Polly had stood up for Coach Warren, Megan experienced a wicked little pleasure at seeing the girl looking a lot more nervous than *she* felt.

"Scared?" Megan asked.

"A little," Polly confessed. "I've never played in a tournament before."

"Neither have I," Megan reminded her.

"But it's different for you. You're a much better player than I am."

Megan regretted her earlier feeling. A warm sensation filled her. That flicker of confidence was growing into a small fire. She put an arm around Polly. "You'll do fine. Just remember everything you learned from me."

"And Coach Warren," Polly added.

Megan removed her arm.

"Look!" Polly cried out. The two girls paused at the top of the slope overlooking the tennis court.

"Wow," Megan breathed. The area had been transformed. A huge banner set up at one end proclaimed WELCOME TO THE FIRST ANNUAL GIRLS' SUMMER CAMP INVITATIONAL TENNIS TOURNAMENT. An equally huge Camp Sunnyside banner decorated the other end. Bleachers had been set up along both sides.

And on those bleachers, girls were gathering. Most of them weren't Sunnyside girls. Megan shaded her eyes and tried to read the names on their tee shirts. "Camp Shining Star. Camp

Blue Lake. Camp Wicki-Wocki. Ick, wouldn't you hate going to a camp with a name like Wicki-Wocki?"

Polly placed a clammy hand on her arm. "Now I'm really getting scared. Do you think they're all competing in the tournament?"

"They couldn't be," Megan reassured her. "There are only two rounds of preliminary games. The others must have come just to watch or cheer on their campers."

Polly shivered. "Do you think they'll boo when my name is announced?"

Megan felt very mature as she tried to comfort Polly. "What if they do? You shouldn't let that bother you. And remember, there can't be more than half a dozen girls from each of the other camps. *We're* on home territory. We've got all of Sunnyside to cheer us on."

"But what if we're playing other Sunnyside girls?" A thought struck Polly, and Megan heard a sharp intake of breath. "Oh, Megan. What if we're playing each other?"

"Don't trouble trouble till trouble troubles you," Megan scolded her. "C'mon, they're drawing the names now. We can find out who we're playing."

The girls ran down the slope to the big blackboard that had been set up just outside the area. It displayed a blank row of lines. The ends of each pair of lines were connected and extended out to make one line. The winner's name would go there. Two counselors were drawing cards from a box and writing names on the board.

"She's writing my name!" Polly exclaimed. The name that followed on the next connected line meant nothing to either of them, and Polly sighed in relief.

Megan's name appeared a second later, followed by the name of her opponent's. "Betsy Drake, Camp Pocahontas," she read out loud.

"That's me," said a soft voice from behind her.

Megan whirled around. A chubby girl of about her own age stood there. She had long straight blonde hair, pulled back in a ponytail, and she smiled nervously.

So this is my rival, Megan thought. It was hard to think of such a sweet-faced girl as an enemy. She returned the smile. "I'm Megan Lindsay."

Betsy Drake looked up at the board. "I guess we're playing each other."

"Looks that way," Megan replied.

There was an awkward moment as the two girls sized each other up. Megan noticed that the hand gripping her racket had white knuckles. She's really scared, Megan thought, and a wave of sympathy passed through her.

"Um, this looks like a nice camp," Betsy offered.

"It's okay," Megan said. "What's Camp Pocahontas like?"

"It's okay," Betsy said. There was another awkward moment. "Well, I guess I'd better go sit with my friends," Betsy said, and she fled.

"She seems nice," Polly said.

Megan nodded. "Yeah. I feel sorry for her."

"Why?"

"Because I'm going to wipe her off the court."

She didn't miss the look of awe that crossed Polly's face, and she beamed. But her face fell with Polly's next words.

"Here comes Coach Warren."

He didn't look any kinder than he had the evening before. He was heading toward the umpire, and for a moment Megan thought he might just pass them by. But she wasn't that fortunate. He paused briefly.

"Good luck," he grunted. Then, to Megan, he added, "Watch your backhand."

Just you wait, Megan replied silently to his

68

back as he walked away. I'll show you. Then she couldn't resist sticking her tongue out at him.

"Megan!" Polly exclaimed in disapproval.

"Let's go find seats," Megan said.

As they climbed the bleachers, Polly said, "You know, working with Coach Warren has really improved my game. Don't you think yours has gotten better?"

"Mine was just fine to begin with," Megan replied shortly. "Look, there's Sarah." She waved to her cabin mate, and Sarah climbed up to join them.

"I won't be playing for at least an hour," Megan told her friend.

"That's okay," Sarah said cheerfully. "We're excused from regular activities if we want to watch the tournament. And anything's better than archery. The others are at the pool, but they'll be here pretty soon."

"I told my cabin mates not to come when I'm playing," Polly said, with an abashed smile. "I was afraid having them here would make me too nervous."

"Nothing makes Megan nervous when she plays tennis," Sarah said.

That was exactly what Megan needed to hear.

Now the fire inside her was blazing, and she couldn't wait to get out on the court.

But she was going to have to be patient. First, there was Ms. Winkle's welcoming speech to get through. The camp director spoke through a microphone. "We're very happy to have all of you here at Camp Sunnyside. It is an honor for us to host the first Girls' Summer Camp Invitational Tennis Tournament. We hope your visit here will be a pleasant one."

Betsy Drake won't find it so pleasant, Megan decided. Then she felt mean for having such thoughts. But that was what playing in a tournament was all about, right? Winning. She just wished she felt more comfortable with that idea. Maybe she could if she stopped thinking of tennis as a game. And considered it something like a—a battle.

Ms. Winkle's speech went on and on, and the crowd was getting restless. But she finally finished, the first two players were announced, and the match began.

One of the Sunnyside girls was playing, and she wasn't bad. But the other girl was much better, and she used more advanced strokes. Along with the others on the bleachers, Megan's head went back and forth with the ball.

"Boy, you could sprain your neck watching this game," Sarah complained. "How long does one last?"

"That depends," Megan said. "A player has to get four points to win a game, and win six games to win a set. If you win two sets, you win a match."

"What if one person wins one set and the other person wins the second set? Is that a tie?"

"No, then they play a third set." She gazed out at the game in progress. "But these guys won't. This match won't last too long," she predicted.

"How can you tell?"

"Because that girl's really good."

"Better than you?" Sarah asked.

Megan grinned cockily. "No."

"Six—love," the umpire called out.

"Love!" Sarah exclaimed. "Is that a score? It sounds very nice!"

"Not to the player who gets it," Megan informed her. "Love means zero points."

The second set resulted in the same score, and the Sunnyside girl was shaking her head ruefully as she shook hands with the winner. "Oh, well, you'll make up for her," Sarah said to Megan. "You too, Polly."

71

The second match went on much longer. The girls were more evenly matched, which was good for them. But they made so few errors that it seemed to take forever before a point was won or lost.

"I'm on next," Polly murmured. She stood up.

"Go out there and knock her dead," Megan said.

Polly shuddered. "That sounds so mean."

"This is a tournament," Megan said sternly. "You have to be mean. Pretend you're going into a battle."

Polly managed a sickly smile, and started down the bleachers. Megan crossed her fingers and hoped her coaching would pay off. Poor Polly didn't look much like a soldier.

Polly got the first serve, and she didn't blow it, but the other girl returned it nicely. Megan watched closely. Polly wasn't playing a very aggressive game, but she was keeping up well with her opponent. Megan applauded when Polly hit a drop shot that the other girl couldn't return.

"I taught her that," she told Sarah proudly, not taking her eyes off the ball. "Wasn't it great?"

"Mmm, great."

Megan glanced at Sarah. She had a book on

her lap. Sarah caught her eye and smiled. "Don't worry. I won't read while you're playing."

Polly's opponent won the first set. But Polly seemed to be gaining confidence, and she won the second. As they went into the third set, Megan stood up.

"I better get down there. I'm on next." She looked around anxiously. "Where are the others?"

Her cabin mates didn't fail her. Just as she was making her way down the bleachers, Katie, Trina, and Erin appeared. Megan barely had time to greet them. Polly's opponent sent a ball out of bounds, and Polly won the match.

Megan scampered down to the court. She watched Polly shake hands with her opponent, and she saw Coach Warren speaking to her. Ignoring him, Megan ran over and gave Polly a quick hug. "Congratulations!"

Polly smiled happily. Then Coach Warren turned. Megan stiffened and waited for his usual "watch your backhand" or "don't play a net game." But he surprised her.

His steely blue eyes bore into hers. "You can win this," he stated bluntly. Then he marched off.

73

Megan stared after him, wondering if she'd heard correctly. Then she realized Betsy Drake was standing there. "Ready to toss?" Betsy asked.

"Go ahead," Megan responded.

Betsy placed the head of the racket on the ground and spun it like a top. Megan called out, "Rough." But the racket fell with the smooth side up. So Betsy got her choice of serving or receiving.

"I'll serve," Betsy said.

Megan took her place deep in the court. With both hands on the racket, she crouched slightly and fixed her eyes on Betsy. Betsy tossed the ball and hit a good, clean serve, clearing the top of the net. Megan let the ball bounce before she returned it.

For a few seconds, they rallied, sending the ball back and forth smoothly. Neither of them had to move too far from their original positions to hit it. Then Megan decided it was time to attack.

She hit a drop shot that just barely cleared the net. It took Betsy by surprise, and she didn't get up to the net fast enough to send it back before the ball bounced twice. Megan got the first point of the game.

Surprise attacks became Megan's strategy for the match. She kept changing the pace, keeping her opponent off balance and guessing. When Betsy got close to the net, Megan forced her into the back court with deep lobs. By switching the direction of the ball, she made Betsy run from one side to the other, up and down the court.

She thought she could almost hear Betsy panting. Every now and then, she caught a glimpse of Betsy's face. Obviously, she wasn't used to playing like this. That look of surprise never left her. Megan won the first set easily.

During the second set, Betsy didn't look surprised anymore. She looked depressed. It was as if she'd given up. She only made halfhearted efforts to return Megan's shots. Megan won game after game.

It was as if no time at all had passed when Megan heard the final score. With the roar of the crowd ringing in her ears like music, Megan ran around to the side and gave a dazed Betsy a quick handshake. Then she was surrounded by her cabin mates.

"You were incredible!" Katie screamed. "I don't even know what you were doing, but it was great!"

Trina, too, was overwhelmed. "I've never seen you play like that before!"

"I never have!" Megan gasped, still a little out of breath. "I just kept telling myself, this isn't a game, it's a war! And it worked!"

"I knew you could do it," Sarah crowed.

"Lindsay!"

Only one person ever called her by her last name. Megan turned to face him. This was it— her moment of triumph. Would he finally smile? Congratulate her? Would he actually admit he was wrong about her?

She left her gang and walked toward him. He gazed at her steadily. Then he spoke. "You know why I'm so hard on you? Why I criticize you more than the others?"

Dumbly, Megan shook her head.

"Because I know you can win. But you're lazy. You can only win if you put everything you've got into it."

Was it her imagination, or did a flicker of a smile cross his face?

"You can see now that I was right," he said. Then he walked away.

Megan scratched her head. That wasn't what she'd expected to hear.

The cabin six girls gathered around her again. "What did he say?" Sarah asked.

"I'm not sure," Megan said. "But I *think* it was a compliment."

"It should be," Katie stated. "You won the game."

"I still can't believe it," Megan murmured.

"Believe it," Erin said. "If you don't, just take a look at your opponent."

Megan followed the direction of Erin's eyes. She saw Betsy Drake sitting on the edge of the bleachers. Another girl wearing a Camp Pocahontas tee shirt had an arm around her. Betsy was crying.

"Let's go," Megan said abruptly. She started out of the area, keeping her back to Betsy. But the image of that tear-streaked face stayed in her mind.

Suddenly, winning wasn't anywhere near as much fun as she'd thought it would be.

Chapter 6

Megan was dreaming. In her dream, she had just won the finals of the tennis tournament. On one side of the court, the bleachers were overflowing with Sunnyside campers, cheering and screaming and throwing confetti in the air. On the other side sat all the girls Megan had beaten. Every one of them had Betsy Drake's face. They weren't cheering. They were all sobbing and wailing, as if the world had just come to an end.

Megan woke up in a cold sweat. It took her a moment to realize she was in her bed in cabin six and that the tournament had only just begun. Above her, she heard rustling. Then Sarah's upside-down head appeared. She was hanging over the side of her upper bunk.

"Are you okay?" she asked in a whisper.

"Yeah," Megan said uncertainly. "Why?"

"You were making noises."

"What kind of noises?"

"Like . . . like whimpering."

Megan scowled. It had been ages since she'd had one of her nightmares. Now this tournament was bringing them on again. "Sorry I woke you," she told Sarah. "Go back to sleep."

Sarah yawned. "It's almost time to get up anyway."

Megan was glad. She didn't want to go back to sleep and risk having another bad dream. Around the room, the other girls began to stir. And a second later, the door to the counselor's room opened and Carolyn stuck her head out.

"Time to get up, girls," she called before retreating back into her room.

With the usual groans and moans, the cabin six girls started getting out of bed. "Who are you playing today, Megan?" Trina asked.

"I don't know yet. I'll be playing whoever won the match after mine yesterday."

"Whoever it is," Katie said, "I feel very sorry for her right now. She doesn't know she's going to be mutilated."

"That's right," Sarah agreed. "She'll end up just like that other girl yesterday. What was her name?"

The name was permanently imprinted on Megan's memory. "Betsy Drake." She grimaced. "I hope this one doesn't cry."

Carolyn came out of her room in time to hear that last remark. "You hope who doesn't cry?"

"The girl I beat today."

"Good grief, Megan," Erin drawled. "You sound awfully sure of yourself."

"It's good for Megan to have confidence," Carolyn noted. She smiled at Megan, but there was a hint of concern in her eyes. "As long as you accept the fact that someday you may come across someone who's better than you are."

"I know that," Megan said. And oddly enough, the thought didn't really bother her. After all, she played Stewart from Camp Eagle all the time. Sometimes she won, sometimes she didn't. But that was what it was all about—you win some, you lose some. That's what made tennis fun—not knowing for sure if you'd play a better game than the other person.

After breakfast, Megan got excused from inspection so she could go directly to the court and find out when her match was scheduled. Other girls were milling around, practicing on the courts and checking the board for their times.

Megan found her name on the board with her

opponent's. Elaine Harrington, Camp South-view. They had the fourth match, which was a relief. At least she'd get to go swimming with the others and do some normal camp stuff.

"Lindsay."

For once, that voice didn't fill her with dread. After her performance yesterday, Gary Warren was bound to be a lot nicer to her.

"Hi," she said, and offered a tentative smile. He didn't return it.

"I'm working with Polly until ten o'clock," he said. "Then I'll want to see you."

"Why?" Megan asked.

"For practice! We need to work on your net game. I watched your opponent yesterday, and she plays close to the net. Be here at ten." With that, he turned and walked away.

Megan clenched her fists. The thought of spending the entire morning practicing volleys and lobs with Coach Warren enraged her. Okay, maybe her net game wasn't perfect, but so what? There was no way she was going to pass up her first free morning in ages. She'd won yesterday, and she'd win today.

She wasn't going to show up, she decided. And she ran off to join her cabin mates at the swimming pool.

"What time is your match?" Katie asked. They were in the stables, brushing off the horses they'd been riding.

"In about twenty minutes," Megan replied.

"Don't you have to go warm up or something?"

"Nah." Megan flapped her arms up and down. "See? I'm real loose." She hadn't felt so relaxed in ages. This was what she had needed—a day of swimming, arts and crafts, horseback riding. Even archery had been almost enjoyable.

"You guys coming to watch my match?"

"Absolutely," Sarah said.

"I don't know," Erin murmured. "I was thinking about French braiding my hair."

Four pairs of eyes gazed at her reproachfully.

"Oh, all right," Erin said.

"Thanks," Megan said sincerely. She needed to have her friends around her. Especially if she came face-to-face with Coach Warren. She didn't want to think about how angry he must have been when she didn't show up at ten.

The bleachers weren't quite as full as they had been the day before. Only half of the original participants were still in the tournament.

Megan took a brief survey of the crowd. She didn't see Coach Warren.

"I have to go check in," she told the others. She went over to the umpire and gave her name. She had just turned away when a slender, pretty girl, with auburn hair pulled back in a knot, stopped her.

"You're Megan Lindsay, right?"

"That's me!"

The girl gave her a friendly smile. "I saw you playing yesterday. You're really good."

"Thank you."

"I'm Elaine Harrington."

It took some effort for Megan to keep on smiling. But at least this one didn't look like the type who cried. "I hope we have a good game."

"Me too," Elaine said. "But I'm going to have a hard time keeping up with you."

Megan shrugged. "Oh well, it's only a game."

Elaine's eyebrows practically reached her hairline. "Only a game? Tennis? For you, maybe. For me, it's my whole life." Her eyes strayed from Megan, and she seemed to be looking off in the distance. When she spoke, her voice was soft. "It's . . . it's my only chance."

Megan was taken aback. She made the game

sound like a life or death situation. "What do you mean?"

Elaine laughed lightly and shook her head. "Oh, you don't want to hear about it."

But now Megan was curious. "Sure I do."

Elaine motioned her away from the crowd. "You see," she began, "my parents . . ." She paused and blinked rapidly. Then she squared her shoulders and took a deep breath, as if she was gathering courage.

"We're very poor. The only reason I'm at summer camp is because a charity sent me."

"Oh." This was a little embarrassing. Megan tried to look appropriately sympathetic, but she didn't know what to say. Her silence felt awkward, so she peered at the girl's name tag. "Do you like Camp Southview?"

"Oh, yes, it's wonderful," Elaine exclaimed in rapture. "There's a real swimming pool and horses and—" she giggled. "You know what I like best?"

"What?"

"The food!"

"Really?" Megan was a little surprised. Camp Sunnyside food was pretty decent, but it wasn't anything to get excited about.

"They give us lots of it," Elaine continued. "I hardly ever get enough to eat at home."

Megan's heart swelled with pity. She couldn't imagine not having enough to eat. "That's awful!"

Elaine nodded. "We don't even have enough money to pay rent. Lately, we've been sleeping in our car."

Megan wished she could think of something cheerful to say. "At least you have a car," she offered lamely.

"It doesn't work," Elaine said. "We can't afford to have it fixed."

Megan's eyes began stinging. This poor girl's life was utterly wretched. At the same time, she couldn't help wondering why Elaine was telling her all this. It didn't have anything to do with tennis.

Elaine was still smiling, but it was a wistful smile. "My parents have pinned all their hopes on me. You see, I'm pretty good at tennis, even though we've never had the money for me to take lessons. My parents want me to become a professional player and start making money." Her eyes were dreamy. "Then we could have a real home and three meals a day."

85

"Gee," Megan whispered. "I hope that happens."

Elaine sighed deeply. "A lot depends on this tournament. There are some important tennis people here—coaches, and people from magazines and television. There's a chance I could get noticed. And maybe, just maybe, someone will want to help me go professional."

"That would be wonderful," Megan said with all her heart. "It would solve all your problems."

Elaine nodded eagerly. Then her smile faded. "Of course, they're not going to notice me if I lose a match."

Suddenly, Megan became uncomfortable. "Well . . . maybe you'll win."

Elaine shook her head sadly. "Not if you play the way you did yesterday." Then she raised her head. "But I'll just do the best I can."

"Yeah. Well, I have to go. See you on the court."

Megan started back toward the bleachers. She was aching inside for Elaine. How awful to be poor, homeless, hungry. Megan shuddered. How could she possibly go out there and beat someone who had such terrible problems? For Megan, winning would be nice. For Elaine . . . it could change her whole life!

She almost hoped Elaine would prove to be an exceptional player, someone impossible to beat. But what if she wasn't? What could Megan do?

Strange ideas popped into her head. It wouldn't be that hard for her. A few missed shots, some bad serves . . . of course, she'd be out of the tournament. And her cabin mates would be disappointed with her. But they'd get over it.

As for the tournament—how would it feel to be knocked out? Well, there'd be no more Coach Warren. No more suffering his barks and criticisms. She could get back into the regular camp routine, have some fun. She could play tennis because she wanted to, not because she had to.

Her thoughts drifted to the regular weekly games she had with Stewart from Camp Eagle. They'd laugh and tease each other, ridiculing their bad shots, admiring their good ones. She liked beating him. But win or lose, they always had a good time. Tournament playing was different.

"Lindsay!"

She froze. All thoughts of Elaine Harrington

dissolved. Coach Warren was coming straight toward her.

"You were supposed to be here at ten."

Megan gulped. "I . . . I forgot."

For a moment, she thought he was going to explode. "You forgot! What's the matter with you?"

Megan had no answer for that. She didn't need one. Coach Warren went right into a lecture.

"Look, Lindsay, you've got a chance to make it in this game. You could be somebody! A champion! You've got the natural talent. You could be one of the major new tennis stars. But you're lazy and sloppy. If you don't start taking this seriously, you're going nowhere. Don't you care?"

A voice came over the loudspeaker. "In the next match, Megan Lindsay of Camp Sunnyside plays Elaine Harrington of Camp Southview."

"I gotta go," Megan blurted out. She fled out to the court.

Elaine spun the racket, and Megan's side turned up. She chose to serve, and went out to the court. Coach Warren's words were still ringing in her ears. She could be a champion, a tennis star. It was a mind-boggling concept. Before she went into her serve, she turned and took a quick look at all the Sunnyside campers watching her with pride.

She tossed the ball and slammed it across the court.

It didn't take long for her to realize that Elaine was good. Very good. And Coach Warren had been right—she did play a net game. For a while Megan tried to go along with her, staying close to the net, sending volleys back and forth. Finally, she managed to score a point when she hit a passing shot past Elaine's reach. From then on, the game was hers. And she won the first set, seven to five.

The familiar rush of triumph filled her. Then she got a glimpse of Elaine's face.

She wasn't crying. But there was despair written all over her face. Then Megan's mind formed a vision. She saw Elaine in rags, her hair matted and dirty, huddled in the back of a beat-up car, unable to sleep because she was hungry.

Suddenly, the thrill of victory was gone. Nothing was worth making another person suffer.

So in the second set, Megan played badly. It wasn't easy for her. A ball would sail past her, and she itched to chase it. But she restrained herself, slowed her pace, and let it bounce twice. She aimed her serves directly into the net. Sometimes they sneaked over, but she managed to accumulate several double faults. Despite her efforts, she won the first game, but then she strengthened her resolve and flailed at the ball helplessly.

It was humiliating, making basic, amateur mistakes in front of all these people. But every time she had the urge to smash a ball, she saw Elaine, hungry and homeless. That kept her going. Elaine took the rest of the games.

They were allowed a break between the second and third sets. When the set was over, Megan went to the table where water was available for the players. Losing didn't feel good, but she'd had a brief look at Elaine. The joy on her face was some comfort. Still, she avoided looking directly at her cabin mates.

She wasn't able to escape all of them, though. Erin followed her to the water table. "I didn't know you were going to play Elaine Harrington."

"Do you know her?" Megan asked.

"Sure. She goes to my school."

Megan was surprised. "I thought you went to a fancy private girls' school."

"Yeah. So does she."

"Oh. I guess she must have a scholarship."

Erin's brow furrowed. "What would she need a scholarship for?"

Erin could be so insensitive, Megan thought. "Because she's poor."

"Poor? Elaine Harrington?" Erin started laughing. "Are you kidding? Her family's one of the richest in town. Their house is bigger than mine! They even have a swimming pool!"

Megan stared at her. "You mean, they don't sleep in a car?"

"Sleep in a car?" Erin rolled her eyes. "Actually, they *could* if they wanted to. Elaine comes to school in a humongous white limousine. Personally, I think that's a little obnoxious, but she's a show-off, and . . ."

Megan had stopped listening. At first, she was completely stunned. Then, her disbelief turned to anger, and it churned inside her. This was outrageous! That little liar had tried to get Megan to throw the match!

Well, the match wasn't over yet. Clutching her racket tightly, Megan stormed back onto the court. Crouching into position, she fixed steely eyes on Elaine. Her opponent must have sensed that something had changed. She looked nervous. And she had good reason to.

Fury fueled Megan's game. She gave it everything she had. She didn't even know she could hit a ball so hard. Her ground strokes were sure and steady, and even her backhand was powerful. She responded to one of Elaine's tricky lobs with an overhead smash that left Elaine helpless. Every time she maneuvered her opponent out of position, she put the ball away, hitting it so well she knew there would be no return.

Elaine fought back, but her efforts were useless. Halfway through the match, Megan knew she could win. And she did.

Elaine stomped off the court, not even bothering with the traditional handshake. Breathless and perspiring, Megan went to the bleachers.

But before she could reach her cabin mates, Coach Warren stopped her. He grabbed her by the shoulders. "You see?" he exclaimed. "You've got it! You've got the killer instinct! You're a destroyer when you want to be!"

They were awful words. *Killer. Destroyer.* But at least he wasn't yelling at her.

"Some of your moves were sloppy," he continued. "And I don't know what was going on in your head in that second set. You need practice and discipline. I want you here tomorrow morning, so we can get you ready for the quarter finals. And no excuses. If you're not here, I'm coming to find you."

He would, too, Megan thought. "Okay," she sighed. "I'll be here."

Chapter 7

"Six–two, Lindsay," boomed the voice over the loudspeaker. From the bleachers, a cheer went up from all the girls wearing Sunnyside tee shirts. Megan shook hands with her opponent, and then flopped down at the end of a bleacher. She didn't even have enough energy to climb up to where her cabin mates were sitting.

She sat there, breathing heavily, and waited for the triumphant thrill of victory to race through her body. But she only felt completely drained.

What a day. From ten in the morning, she'd practiced with Coach Warren. Over and over, she'd hit ground strokes from every spot on the court. She'd passed volleys back and forth with him. She'd worked on her backhand. She'd hit approach shots, overhead shots, every shot that had ever been played in the game of tennis. And all the time, Coach Warren kept yelling, "Harder! Faster! Keep your wrist firm! Bend your elbow!"

She didn't even get to join her cabin mates for lunch. Coach Warren had brought sandwiches, and while they ate he lectured her on everything she had done wrong.

She had to admit that the intense practice session had paid off. Today, in the quarter final, she'd played better than ever. Then why wasn't she floating in ecstasy?

"Excuse me. Megan Lindsay?"

Megan looked up to see a tall, attractive woman in a crisp jumpsuit standing in front of her. Under her arm was a little portable tape recorder.

"Yes, I'm Megan Lindsay."

"Can I talk to you for a minute?"

"Sure."

The woman sat down beside her. Megan watched with apprehension as she switched on her tape recorder.

"What's that for?"

"I'm from *Racket* magazine," the woman explained. "I've been interviewing some of you girls for an article we're preparing on budding

95

tennis stars. And from the way you played to-day, you certainly qualify. Now, to begin with, how long have you been playing tennis?"

For the next few minutes, Megan answered a lot of questions. She told the reporter her age, her address, where she played back home, and why she got interested in tennis.

"How many hours a week do you play tennis?" she asked.

"That depends," Megan replied. "I mean, sometimes I play a lot. And sometimes I don't play at all."

The woman seemed to find that odd. "But aren't you on any kind of regular schedule?"

"No. I just play when I feel like it."

"You must take regular lessons."

Megan shook her head. "Sometimes I sign up for a series of after-school lessons at the community center back home. But then I'll miss a lot of them because of other things I want to do after school."

The reporter appeared to be puzzled. "But surely, you must realize that becoming a serious tennis player requires a major commitment."

Megan looked at her blankly. "Huh?"

"You've got a great deal of potential. You

should be getting intensive training. Of course, then you'd have to be willing to make sacrifices. Are you prepared for that?"

"What kind of sacrifices?"

The woman made a sweeping gesture. "Professional tennis players have to give up many of the ordinary things young people do. Like hobbies and school activities and parties . . . do you think you could do that? Devote your life to tennis?"

Megan considered that. "What about gymnastics?"

"Gymnastics!"

"Yeah, I'm on the team at my school. Would I have to give that up?"

"Of course! You wouldn't have the time, and you shouldn't run the risk of injury. Now, let me ask you this. What are your goals as a tennis player? Do you see yourself playing at Wimbledon or the U.S. Open in a few years?"

Megan scratched her head. "I don't know."

The reporter was beginning to look annoyed. "Megan, why do you play tennis?"

Megan searched for an answer. "It's . . . it's fun."

At that, the woman shut off her tape recorder. "Thank you, dear," she said hurriedly, and set off in search of other players. Megan was immediately surrounded by her cabin mates.

"Who was that?" Katie asked.

"A reporter from some tennis magazine."

"How exciting!" Trina responded. "Are they going to write about you?"

"I don't know." Personally, Megan doubted it. She didn't think the reporter found her very interesting. "You guys want to go get some ice cream or something?" she asked hopefully.

"Megan!" Erin exclaimed. "How can you think of ice cream when you just won the quarter final? You're going to be in the semifinals tomorrow!"

"And after you win that, you'll be in the finals," Sarah added. "Aren't you excited?"

"Wow," Erin murmured. "You'll start playing in professional games soon. Maybe you'll be a star, like that Gabriella Sabatini. Did you know she's a millionaire?"

Megan stirred restlessly. "Yeah. Listen, you guys, I don't want to think about tennis right now, okay?"

She couldn't blame them for looking puzzled. When had she ever not wanted to talk, play, think about tennis?

"She's getting temperamental," Erin stated to the others. "All big stars get that way."

"Okay," Katie said. "Let's go get ice cream."

But just as Megan hopped up, she saw Coach Warren striding toward her. Her cabin mates stepped back respectfully.

"You were good today," he told Megan. "But you spent too much time in the back court. If your opponent had known anything about drop shots she could have put you away. We need to work on your net game."

Megan nodded in resignation. "Okay. Tomorrow."

"No, the semifinals have been scheduled for the morning, with the final in the afternoon. We'll have to work this evening."

"This evening?" Megan had the awful feeling that she was on the verge of tears. "I can't practice this evening!"

"Why not?"

"I can't! I just can't!"

"But you need the practice," Coach Warren argued. "Do you know who you're playing tomorrow?"

Megan hadn't watched the other quarter final games. "No."

"Jackson."

99

It took Megan a moment to remember who "Jackson" was. "You mean, Polly? I'm playing Polly?"

"She won her quarter final. And she looked good out there."

"I can beat Polly," Megan stated flatly. "She's younger than me. I taught her half the strokes she knows, anyway."

Coach Warren wasn't impressed. "I just told you, she was good today."

Megan was amazed by the sudden surge of courage that filled her. "Well, you just said *I* was good. I don't want any more practice, I don't need any more practice, and I'm not going to practice! And you can't make me!" With that, she turned away and started walking rapidly out of the area.

Her cabin mates ran to catch up with her. "Megan!" Trina gasped. "How could you be so rude?"

"That's not like you at all!" Sarah chimed in.

"I don't care," Megan raged. "I'm sick of him. I'm sick of all of this."

Katie's mouth fell open. "You're sick of tennis?"

"No! It's just . . ." She struggled to find the words to express what she was feeling. "It's just that everyone keeps talking about how serious this is. That reporter said I had to give up everything to play tennis. Coach Warren keeps telling me how I have to be a killer and destroy my opponent. But I'm not like that! I just want . . . I just want to play tennis!"

"But that's what you're doing," Erin said in bewilderment.

Megan groaned. She wasn't getting through to them. But how could she, when she didn't understand herself? At least they all looked sympathetic.

"You shouldn't have to practice tonight if you really don't want to," Trina said.

"I don't. You know what I want to do tonight? I want to have some fun. Some real fun. I want us to do something silly and crazy, like we used to do."

"You know," Katie said thoughtfully, "that could be arranged. I was talking to Melissa in cabin seven. They got some huge box of goodies this morning, and they're going to have a lights-out party. Melissa invited us."

"What about their counselor?" Erin asked.

"You know what she's like," Katie said. "She goes to sleep early with earplugs. They get away

101

with murder in there. They stay up and play music and everything."

"Wait a minute," Trina objected. "Megan can't go to a lights-out party tonight. She has to play tennis early in the morning. She's going to need a good night's sleep."

"Trina's right," Sarah said. "Maybe they can have the party tomorrow night, after the tournament's over." She beamed at Megan."Then it could be a victory party."

"Yeah, that's a good idea," Katie agreed. "We'll do something else tonight. Maybe play Monopoly. How does that sound, Megan?"

Megan's smile was halfhearted. Playing Monopoly was nothing special. But it was better than an evening of practice.

After dinner, Carolyn disappeared into her room for a while. When she emerged, the girls greeted her with oohs and ahhs.

"You look fabulous!" Erin said. "I love your hair that way."

Carolyn struck a pose for them. "I haven't had a dress on in so long, it feels like a costume."

"Where are you going?" Sarah asked.

"I'm staying with a girlfriend in Pine Ridge.

We're going to dinner at the Pine Ridge Inn, and then to a play."

"That sounds glamorous," Erin sighed.

"Who's staying with us tonight?" Katie asked.

"Donna. She'll be here any minute."

The girls exchanged pleased smiles, and Megan knew why. Donna had stayed with them before on Carolyn's nights off. She always stayed in the counselor's room, with a book and headphones clamped over her ears. They could do anything they wanted when Donna was there. The Monopoly game could go on all night.

The door opened and Donna burst in. "Hi! I'm not late, am I?"

"Right on time," Carolyn told her. "You guys be good and don't get into any trouble, okay?"

"Donna wouldn't know if we did," Sarah whispered to Megan. Sure enough, the minute Carolyn left the cabin, Donna said, "I'll be in here if you need anything." She disappeared into the room, and Megan knew they wouldn't see her again until morning.

"Let's set up the Monopoly board," Katie suggested. Just as Trina was dealing out the money, their door opened. Melissa, from cabin seven, came in. "Just wanted to tell you we're

103

going to have the party tonight. The cake will get stale if we don't."

"What kind of cake is it?" Megan asked.

"Chocolate with white chocolate chips and mocha icing."

Sarah clutched herself and groaned mournfully. "That sounds heavenly."

"And there are peanut crunch cookies, caramel brownies, barbecue potato chips, doughnuts with custard filling—"

"Stop!" Katie shrieked. "I can't stand it!"

"And there's tons of everything," Melissa said. "We're not going to be able to eat it all."

"Thanks for inviting us," Trina said, "but we can't come. Megan has to go to bed early."

Megan felt terrible. "You guys can go without me. I don't mind staying alone." She hoped she sounded like she really meant that. But the thought of sleeping alone in the cabin gave her the creeps. Not to mention the fact that she'd be missing the party.

"Not without you," Sarah said stoutly.

"Okay," Melissa said. "But you're missing a good time. Karen's got all the New Kids on the Block tapes."

Megan gritted her teeth. It wasn't fair. Why should they have to miss this party? Why couldn't she enjoy herself, have a good time, like she used to? Melissa was halfway out the door when Megan called, "Wait!"

Melissa paused and turned back.

"We're coming," Megan declared.

"Megan, you can't!" Trina said.

Megan jumped off the bed and faced them all. "Look, I can beat Polly blindfolded and with one hand tied behind my back. I don't need much sleep."

She could tell they were tempted. Sarah looked positively torn. "Megan, I still don't think it's a good idea."

But Katie and Erin were ready to give in. "I can bring my Madonna tapes," Katie offered.

"And I'll bring my makeup," Erin said. "We can do makeovers on each other."

"Cool!" Melissa said. "C'mon over in a couple of hours. Our counselor will be asleep by then." She left, and the girls returned to their game.

But Trina was still eyeing Megan with concern. "Are you sure you want to do this?"

Megan nodded fervently. "I've been working so hard. I deserve a good time."

"Of course you do," Sarah replied. "But what about the tournament?"

Megan put her hands over her ears. "I don't

want to hear one more word about that tournament! We're going to that party. And we're going to have fun!"

It *was* fun. The goodies were every bit as spectacular as Melissa had promised. Tapes blared from a cassette player, and the girls danced. Megan danced more than anyone. She wolfed down brownies and potato chips and doughnuts, and she roared with laughter as Erin put makeup on Katie and turned her into a punk. They played hearts, and they gossiped, and they giggled like maniacs.

It wasn't until Sarah fell asleep on the floor that the girls realized it was almost two in the morning. Groaning from exhaustion and too much food, the girls pulled Sarah off the floor and dragged themselves back to their own cabin.

Barely a word was spoken while they got ready for bed. Megan didn't even bother to undress. She collapsed on her bed and fell asleep.

It seemed like only a minute later she began dreaming that Donna was standing in the cabin, yelling "Wake up! Time to get up, girls!"

She forced her eyes open a crack. It wasn't a dream.

Chapter 8

It couldn't be morning. It just couldn't be. Megan felt like she hadn't even been to sleep yet. She struggled to pull herself up on her elbows. "What time is it?"

"Eight o'clock," Katie croaked. She didn't sound very wide awake either.

Megan's brain was fogged over. "Eight o'clock," she repeated stupidly.

"And you're playing tennis at ten," Trina said. "Megan, are you okay?"

"Am I okay?" Megan echoed. "I don't know." She was dimly aware of a peculiar sensation. "My stomach hurts."

"I'm not surprised," Erin commented. "You only ate about a dozen brownies."

Megan swung her legs over the side of her bed and groaned. Every bone in her body ached, including the ones in her head. Gingerly, she got up.

Sarah was watching her worriedly. "Why don't you take a shower? That'll make you feel better."

"Yeah, I will." Feeling as if she was walking in slow motion, Megan padded into the bathroom.

The shower didn't make her feel any better, just cleaner. Her mind seemed to be full of cotton wool, and her arms and legs were made of lead. Somehow, she managed to make it to the dining hall, but the sight of breakfast didn't improve her condition. If anything, the smell of bacon and eggs made her stomach turn over.

Luckily, Carolyn wasn't there, and Donna was preoccupied with her book. But her cabin mates noticed how she was feeling.

"Are you sure you're okay?" Trina asked. "Your face is practically green."

"I'm fine," Megan lied.

Sarah was concerned too. "Do you think you'll be able to play tennis?"

Megan felt as if she could barely move. But she wasn't about to admit it. "Of course I can play tennis," she said, with all the indignation she could muster. "Besides, like I told you, it's

108

not going to be a rough game. Polly's two years younger than me! I could beat her in my sleep!"

She was aware of all her cabin mates, even Erin, giving her skeptical looks. But she just pushed her food around her plate, and ignored them.

Not being a regular cabin counselor, Donna forgot about cleanup and inspection, which was fine with the girls. After breakfast, Megan trailed after the others as they went to the courts. She couldn't remember ever feeling so tired in her life. Her foggy mind kept drifting. She tried to think about Polly, and remember what her strengths and weaknesses were. But nothing registered in her head.

It would feel strange, playing against Polly. She was such a sweet kid. And Polly really cared about tennis a lot. She probably didn't expect to win against an older and more experienced player. But Megan only hoped Polly wouldn't feel too hurt when she lost.

When they arrived at the courts, the other semifinal couple was playing. Megan wanted to watch, so she could see who she'd be playing that afternoon in the finals. But her eyes wouldn't focus. Everything seemed hazy.

"Megan!"

Megan turned to Sarah. "Huh?"

"I've called your name three times! Are you in a trance or what?"

Megan managed a feeble imitation of a smile. "I'm concentrating on the match."

"Oh." The reply seemed to satisfy her. "She's concentrating on the match," Sarah told the others.

"Hi, Megan." Polly stood there, twisting her racket in her hands.

"Hi, Polly."

"This feels weird, doesn't it?"

"Huh?"

"Playing each other. In a tournament. Doesn't it feel strange to you?"

"Yeah," Megan admitted. "I guess it does feel a little weird."

Polly bit her lip. "Megan . . . whatever happens, I mean, whoever wins or loses . . . we'll still be friends, right?"

"Sure we will," Megan replied. "It's just a game, Polly." Her eyes were starting to clear a little. She could see Carla and Leslie climbing up the bleachers toward them.

"We came to watch," Leslie announced. "Only we don't know who to root for."

Megan's head was beginning to clear too. She

grinned. "You could split up. One of you could root for me and one of you could root for Polly."

"But how do we choose who gets who?" Carla asked.

Polly giggled nervously. "You could switch after the first set."

"The tournament's going to be over today, right?" Leslie asked Megan. "Can we start having lessons again tomorrow?"

Megan looked at her closely. "Do you really want to?"

Leslie shrugged. Megan switched her focus to Carla. The small girl gave an unenthusiastic nod.

Megan shook her head. "No, you don't. Neither of you really enjoy playing tennis. Carla, you've just got to get up the nerve to tell your father tennis isn't your game. Maybe he'll be disappointed, but he'll get over it. And Leslie, why don't you find something you actually *like* doing that you can beat your classmate at?"

It was the longest speech she'd made all day, and the effort made her head throb. But she was pleased to see both girls looking thoughtful.

"Look!" Polly said suddenly.

The match was over. Megan tried to get a

good look at the winner. She was tall. That could be a problem.

She heard a voice call out, "The next match will be played by Megan Lindsay, Camp Sunnyside, and Polly Jackson, Camp Sunnyside."

"Here we go," Polly said in a high-pitched squeak.

Megan rose. Then, on a whim, she put her arm around Polly. "Let's give them a good show," she said. And they went down to the court together.

Megan spun her racket. Polly called "Smooth" but it came up rough. "I'll serve," Megan said.

Walking across the court, she was aware that her racket felt unusually heavy. Who would have thought a lack of sleep would weaken her arms? She decided to make this serve an easy one, not just for her own sake, but for Polly's too. She wanted Polly to be able to return it, to give her confidence.

She went into a flat serve, aiming the ball right where Polly was positioned. But the ball didn't get there. It hit the net. Megan was surprised. She hardly ever blew a serve.

She tossed the ball again. And she watched in amazement as it made a beeline for the net.

112

The game had barely started, and she'd already lost a point.

It was an omen of things to come. Nothing was working for her. She'd run to meet a ball, and totally miscalculate the distance. She'd approach a ball, swing her racket, and not even make contact. She'd attempt an overhead smash, and send the ball way over the boundary line. It was unbelievable. Her brain was sending messages to her arms and legs, but her limbs weren't receiving them.

Polly, on the other hand, was at her best. She tore all over the court, taking advantage of Megan's weaknesses and showing strengths Megan didn't even know she had. She had no problem at all winning the first set.

Megan tried as hard as she could to concentrate in the second set. And she was better. Her arms and legs started to obey her brain. She even managed a few unreturnable ground strokes. But she still wasn't playing the way she could have played if she wasn't exhausted, if she wasn't spaced out, if she didn't have a rumbling stomach and a headache. She managed, with every ounce of the little energy she had in her, to take two games. But Polly took the rest. And she deserved to.

Even so, it was something of a shock to hear the final score announced. And to realize she had lost. Dazed and dizzy, she went to the end of the net to shake hands with Polly. The younger girl actually looked frightened, as if she was afraid Megan was going to bang her on the head with her racket. So Megan put a little extra warmth in her smile, and took Polly's hand in both of hers. It wasn't that hard. She really was happy for her.

Then Polly was engulfed by a group of shrieking girls from her cabin. Megan went to the bleachers to face her own cabin mates.

Their expressions were all pretty similar—sad, sympathetic, concerned. They were waiting for Megan to cry. But Megan didn't feel like crying. She wasn't exactly happy. On the other hand, she couldn't really say she was miserable. If she had to give a name to what she was feeling, she'd call if relief. The tournament was over for her. Now she could go back to playing tennis for the right reasons.

"It's okay, you guys," she told her cabin mates. "You can't win them all."

"You don't have to be brave with us," Sarah said. "We know you're feeling bad."

"Not *that* bad," Megan said. "No worse than I feel when Stewart beats me."

"But this was a tournament!" Erin exclaimed.

Megan shrugged. "I guess it was just another game to me."

Erin didn't buy that. "But you could have become famous! You could have been a big tennis star!"

"Erin, that's not what I play tennis for."

"Lindsay!"

Megan heaved a huge sigh. She was going to have to face him sooner or later. At least Coach Warren didn't look angry—just disgusted.

"That was pathetic," he said. "What happened to you? Where was your killer instinct?"

"I guess I don't have one," Megan replied. "Look, I'm sorry if you wasted your time with me. But I don't want to be a killer. I do love tennis. But I love lots of things. And I'm not going to give them up for tennis."

He shook his head regretfully. "Then you'll never make it professionally."

"Guess not," Megan said. "But that's okay with me. I can always play for fun."

"Fun!" He acted like she'd just said a dirty

word. Then he threw up his hands and left to join the crowd around Polly.

He doesn't understand, Megan thought. As she took in the puzzled expressions of her cabin mates, she realized that they didn't really understand either.

But she did. And that was all that mattered.

MEET THE GIRLS FROM CABIN SIX IN

CAMP SUNNYSIDE FRIENDS

#12) THE TENNIS TRAP 76184-X ($2.95 US/$3.50 Can)

(#11) THE PROBLEM WITH PARENTS
76183-1 ($2.95 US/$3.50 Can)

(#10) ERIN AND THE MOVIE STAR 76181-5 ($2.95 US/$3.50 Can)

(#9) THE NEW-AND-IMPROVED SARAH
76180-7 ($2.95 US/$3.50 Can)

(#8) TOO MANY COUNSELORS 75913-6 ($2.95 US/$3.50 Can)

(#7) A WITCH IN CABIN SIX 75912-8 ($2.95 US/$3.50 Can)

(#6) KATIE STEALS THE SHOW 75910-1 ($2.95 US/$3.50 Can)

(#5) LOOKING FOR TROUBLE 75909-8 ($2.95 US/$3.50 Can)

(#4) NEW GIRL IN CABIN SIX 75703-6 ($2.95 US/$3.50 Can)

(#3) COLOR WAR! 75702-8 ($2.50 US/$2.95 Can)

(#2) CABIN SIX PLAYS CUPID 75701-X ($2.50 US/$2.95 Can)

(#1) NO BOYS ALLOWED! 75700-1 ($2.50 US/$2.95 Can)

MY CAMP MEMORY BOOK 76081-9 ($5.95 US/$7.95 Can)

CAMP SUNNYSIDE FRIENDS SPECIAL:
CHRISTMAS REUNION 76270-6 ($2.95 US/$3.50 Can)

A CAST OF CHARACTERS
TO DELIGHT THE HEARTS
OF READERS!

BUNNICULA   51094-4/$2.95 U.S./$3.50 CAN.
James and Deborah Howe, illustrated by Alan Daniel
The now-famous story of the vampire bunny, this ALA
Notable Book begins the light-hearted story of the small
rabbit the Monroe family find in a shoebox at a Dracula
film. He looks like any ordinary bunny to Harold the dog.
But Chester, a well-read and observant cat, is suspicious
of the newcomer, whose teeth strangely resemble
fangs...

HOWLIDAY INN   69294-5/$3.50 U.S./$3.95 CAN.
James Howe, illustrated by Lynn Munsinger
The continued "tail" of Chester the cat and Harold the dog
as they spend their summer vacation at the foreboding
Chateau Bow-Wow, a kennel run by a mad scientist!

THE CELERY STALKS   69054-3/$2.95 U.S./$3.50 CAN.
AT MIDNIGHT
James Howe, illustrated by Leslie Morrill
Bunnicula is back and on the loose in this third hilarious
novel featuring Chester the cat, Harold the dog, and the
famous vampire bunny.

NIGHTY-NIGHTMARE   70490-0/$3.50 U.S./$3.95 CAN.
James Howe, illustrated by Leslie Morrill
Join Chester the cat, Harold the dog, and Howie the other
family dog as they hear the tale of how Bunnicula was
born while they are on an overnight camping trip full of
surprises!